DAYS OF FADING DREAMS

MATT LARKIN

DAYS OF FADING DREAMS

Runeblade Saga: Book Four

MATT LARKIN

This is a work of fiction. Names, characters, organizations, businesses, places, events and incidents either are the product of the author's imagination or are used fictitiously.

Published by Incandescent Phoenix Books

mattlarkinbooks.com

CONTENTS

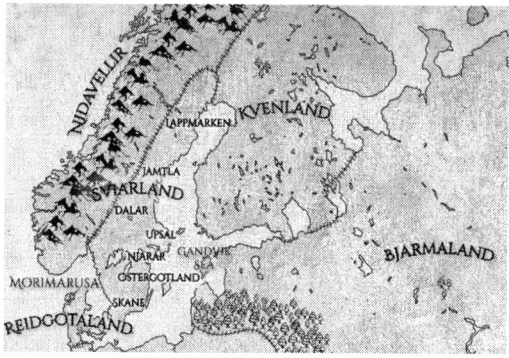

For more maps, join the Skalds' Tribe and get a free codex of
The Ragnarok Era:

https://www.mattlarkinbooks.com/go-runeblade/

PROLOGUE

*T*hough far from a perfect world, Midgard was the only one men had, and thus, Odin found himself forced to preserve it through any means available. If Ragnarok could not be averted, perhaps it might be delayed, or—at the least—won.

And thus he found himself forever wandering, seeking every bit of knowledge with which he might forearm himself against the coming battle. Midgard was vast and filled with myriad secrets oft lost to the ages, or nigh to it.

As now, when he walked the frozen lake shores of Kalevala in Kvenland. He had come here before, of course, several times. For here lay the extreme fringes of the human world, a land where some vestiges of arcane lore yet remained, passed down among shamans and wandering wizards.

True knowledge was rare, of course. As nigh as Odin could tell, only a handful of sorcerers yet walked Midgard, and the better part of those he was forced to count among his many enemies. But Odin had met a few wizards in Kvenland before and made the acquaintance of one he now sought. A song-crafter, the wizard called himself, a practitioner of galdr. Odin's studies with Freya had only scraped the surface of the Art, so he could only assume the songs another means of invocation.

And yet the mastery Väinämöinen had demonstrated, his ability to affect and influence the world through his galdr—they had been uncanny. An ability Odin would need himself if he was to win Ragnarok.

And so he walked the lake shores in Kalevala, stalked the woodlands, and scoured the hills. Idunn's apples had made him immortal and, still, he had never enough time. Too many places he needed to be, too many moves to make on the tafl board. For all his gifts and all his power, he could not be in two places at once—though Sleipnir's speed did help him cover great distances in but a few days—and every moment he spent here was one lost to other opportunities.

Wandering the wilds alone oft gave him overmuch time to think, to lose himself in such musings. It almost made him sympathetic toward Loki, who himself must nigh to have drowned in his endless, perilous memories. Men thought them gods and still could not begin to imagine the burdens of immortality.

At last, Odin cracked a slight smile. Upon the shore of a pristine lake, there sat the man himself, arms draped over his knees, gazing out as if he had not a care in this world. Odin had not looked upon Väinämöinen in a number of winters, yet the man seemed little changed. Maybe a few more hints of gray in his long blond hair and beard. The man rocked in time with the breeze, humming to himself, even when he turned his blue-eyed gaze upon Odin.

"I have sought you long," Odin said, approaching the

song-crafter's side before settling down beside him. "You are sometimes not so easy to find."

"When two wanderers pass each other by and chance to meet or chance to miss, do you see the hand of urd or but the winds of luck?" He spoke almost in rhythm as well, as though making up words to a song even while conversing. From another, Odin would have misliked it as an affectation bordering on hubris. From Väinämöinen, though, his voice was nigh to hypnotic, so crystal clear and lilting, one was tempted to close one's eyes and become lost in the words.

"I have thought oft of the last time we spoke." Odin shook his head. "In my haste, my ... *desperation* to find a way to reach Alfheim, I paid but little heed to aught else around me. Overlooking, perhaps, the gift you were given, and the aid such song-craft might offer in the coming struggle."

"And the vagrant returns from long wanderings, seeking that which he vainly left behind, as if all things were not altered by the passing of time. But we cannot go back to the places we have known and call them the same. The very effort of it promises bitter disappointment."

Odin cleared his throat. "Because the places change?" Väinämöinen stared at him in that wry, infuriating way Odin had come to associate with Loki.

"Because *we* change."

Odin sighed. "Be that as it may, I have not come here to bandy riddles, wizard. I seek knowledge of your song-craft. Teach me of the galdr, and I will offer you riches beyond the dreams of other men."

"And in so offering you imagine all men seek naught but wealth. A song then, a lesson to be well heeded, for it shall not be soon repeated."

Odin stared at the lake. Väinämöinen seemed a difficult

tutor, but then all his instructors in the Art had been. Perhaps that bespoke the difficulty of imparting the subject itself, or, perhaps, the way that subject altered the minds of those who dared delve into it.

Beside him, the other man began to sing, his voice high and clear, echoing off the pristine hills and rolling over the waters. He sang of the birth of life, emerging from the sky and the sea. He sang of the dying of ages, and the rising of tides to swallow the ungrateful land. He sang of an era inundated by an unending ocean.

The more he sang, the deeper Odin felt himself falling into a meditative trance. If he could but isolate the source of Väinämöinen's power, if he could understand the verses, he might ... might ...

Waters rose around Odin's feet and pooled about his arse, chilly, nigh to freezing. He felt their icy touch, but couldn't make himself care enough to pull away from the song.

And Väinämöinen sang of a world drowned for its crimes and washed clean to begin anew. A hope, perhaps, that through strife the darkness might itself be held back.

The waters had risen to Odin's neck and held him fast like quicksand. They pulled him out into the lake and under, deep into icy submersion.

"Forgive me, King of the Aesir. But you too have your crimes which must be washed clean. If a single hand falls upon every piece, if all the world becomes a tafl board controlled by one, then, would another player wish to join the match, he would need pry free a pawn from the one's greedy grasp. And in the end, even the greedy player might appreciate that a game is most interesting with skilled opponents."

The lake wrapped around Odin and drew him down, into the sludge at its base. Some dim part of his mind expected to drown, but he found the thought hardly scared him.

Peace was his at long last.

PART I

Twelfth Moon
Year 29, Age of the Aesir
Eight Moons After *Days of Frozen Hearts*

espite being well into summer, a chill breeze swept over the plains, prickling Hervor's skin and billowing her hair. Very soon they would reach Holmgard. Already they'd seen small outlying villages claimed by the faltering kingdom.

Hervor had almost finished packing up the campsite, and still Starkad slumbered. The man had never been one to sleep soundly, but these days Hervor would swear to Odin that things had grown worse. Starkad moaned, thrashed from side to side on his bedroll, fitful.

All right, then, that was about enough of that.

Hervor knelt beside him, grabbed his shoulder and shook. "Come on now. Höfund will be back any moment."

Starkad jerked awake. Before Hervor could even open her mouth, his hand was around her throat. He heaved her backward, his grip strong as a bear's. It was just an instant, and then his eyes widened and he released her.

"I ..."

Odin's balls. Hervor backed away, rubbed her throat. Glowered at Starkad.

"Hervor, I ... You caught me by surprise."

"It's getting worse."

Starkad said naught. Instead, the man climbed to his feet, then wandered off away from the campsite, no doubt to take a piss.

Hervor grumbled under her breath. The past fortnight had been about as much fun as storming the gates of Hel. Whatever had gotten into Starkad, he had clamped down about it, tighter than a troll's arse.

He was keeping things from her again. Despite their oaths to one another, the promises they had made in Godmund's hall, he held back now, as he had done in the past. Every step they drew closer together, he always took one away from her as well. Was that his curse?

Or was he just a colossal arse?

And Hel take her, *she* still couldn't tell him everything either. Some things must remain buried if they were to have a chance at happiness together.

The man returned a moment later, face wet from the nearby stream. He shook himself, then set about helping pack without another word.

Fine. Whatever.

Hervor left the campfire going just in case Höfund managed to catch aught worth eating. The half jotunn had a knack for hunting down game in even the most inhospitable of climes.

Hervor watched Starkad's back as he worked, as he bustled about as if she hadn't done most everything before he woke. How could things have turned out like this? Of course, she couldn't tell him everything, but *he* didn't know that. So he ought to have told her what so vexed him of late.

Whatever beset him, it was her burden to bear as well,

so long as they remained together. As they had sworn they would.

She opened her mouth, not even sure what she wanted to say. It didn't matter anyway. Before she could form words, Höfund came tromping down the hill toward their campsite.

The man bore a skinned snow rabbit in one hand, a massive grin on his face. After settling by the fire, he drove the carcass onto a spit and shoved it over the flames, his smile starting to fade as he took in her and Starkad.

Even when Höfund had cooked the rabbit, even when they had eaten, no one said aught. Until Höfund as well fell glum and melancholy.

THEY HAD LEFT Höfund's father's keep at the break of summer. Had passed through the frozen wastes of Jotunheim, and into the seemingly endless wilds of Bjarmaland. And now, finally, after long moons of travel, Holmgard drew into view.

As towns went, it wasn't overmuch to look at. Small, and seeming to dwindle rather than grow as the years passed by. Gylfi's colony here was clearly faltering. Another generation, perhaps, and it would fall to the encroaching lands of the jotunn kings. Maybe Hervor's paternal grandfather was to blame, or maybe urd. Breaches in the Midgard Wall allowed the chaos of Jotunheim to seep back into the world of men.

That chaos preyed upon the men of Bjarmaland first. Crushed their kingdoms and took their sons and daughters as slaves.

Long travels across Midgard and beyond left Hervor with one inescapable conclusion: the world was doomed.

The forces of chaos closed in on all sides. The mists brought the merciless dead in to crush the living. Jotunnar breached the wall, claimed more and more lands as their own. And vaettir lurked on the outskirts, preying on the bodies and souls of hapless men and women.

All that remained to Hervor now was to get what she could from life, and hope that the final end came long after her time had passed.

Starkad thrived on these adventures, craved them, maybe even needed them. But to Hervor's mind, knowledge of what lay just beyond the lands of man did more harm than good.

Wudga had opened Starkad's mind to the Otherworlds with that Eitr and—though Starkad never said much of it—he'd mentioned he had some semblance of the Sight. What that meant ... well, she remained yet uncertain, save that uncanny insights now seemed to guide her lover at times. And that the dreams grew ever worse.

Looking into the Otherworlds ... Damn. Small wonder Starkad had so many fucking nightmares. For all Hervor could tell, those realms were made of terror.

Höfund gaped at the wall surrounding Holmgard. "Didn't know humans could build that big."

Hervor scoffed and shook her head.

Starkad answered before she could. "Naught special here. Even among modern men, this is but a small settlement. The ruins built by the Old Kingdoms put such constructions to shame. If you come with us, back to Sviarland, you'll see far grander designs, if oft in ruin."

Höfund worked his jaw a moment, then shook his head. "Reckon I ought to have a look around human lands what's nigh to the Midgard Wall first. Don't know as I'm ever going back to Father's lands, but just the same. Best to know what lies close at hand."

What did that mean? Was Höfund actually considering reporting back to his father about the state of Holmgard? Of all Bjarmaland? Would Godmund bring his jotunnar here, for conquest?

In Bjarmaland, they had passed numerous petty king-doms controlled by jotunn lords. Urd aside, Hervor would hate to see that befall Holmgard. Besides, Godmund had seemed content with his lands in Utgard.

Either way, though, Hervor needed to return to Sviar-land. More than a year had passed since she had last seen her homeland, since she had spoken to her grandfather. He would no doubt be wondering if she yet lived.

The gate guards let them through the wall though they cast a wary eye upon Höfund. No surprise there, given the half jotunn towered over the tallest of men. Easily seven feet tall. The guards knew Starkad, and no one who knew him tried to bar his way.

Beyond the gates she and Starkad bid Höfund farewell. Godmund's son had been an interesting traveling compan-ion, maybe even a friend. Part of Hervor was sorry to see him go. But they'd had this conversation before. Höfund insisted on seeing all of the world of men, one kingdom at a time, and she and Starkad had business that would not wait.

Starkad led her toward the waterfront where Hervor heard the shouts of men loading and unloading ships, preparing to voyage across the Gandvik Sea to trade with her homeland. In the heart of summer, trade was up, but it would not last long. And they needed to be on one of those ships.

"I'm going to try to find passage to Upsal," Starkad said.

Hervor grimaced. Thrice damned Upsal was the last

kingdom in Sviarland she much wanted to visit. "What about Ostergotland?"

Starkad shook his head. "I gave my oath to Gylfi. I must hand over the runeblade without any further delay. We lingered too long in Jotunheim as it is. Upsal puts us closer to Dalar."

It also put them in the kingdom of the godsdamned Ynglings, even if Hervor had declared her vengeance against them sated. But she could hardly tell Starkad the reason for her dislike of Upsal. And, though she mislike him, King Aun had sheltered them last year, offering naught but gracious hospitality.

Hervor sighed. It seemed she wasn't going home quite yet after all.

2

*I*n Upsal, Ale of Reidgotaland had ousted King Aun. It ought not to have surprised Starkad. Aun had been little warlike from all Starkad had seen, and he'd heard the man had suffered defeats from even old Healf-dene, Hrothgar's father, years back, when he was but a mere jarl. Still, Aun was wise and had offered friendship to Starkad. Under other circumstances, Starkad might have sought the man out from exile and tried to help him. Maybe when his business with Gylfi was at last complete, he could yet do so.

From Upsal, they pushed hard for Dalar and for Gylfi's hall. Starkad misliked having an unfulfilled oath, especially to a man like Gylfi. Sorcerers touched the Otherworlds and, in so doing, made themselves something other than human.

No doubt many would have thought much the same of Starkad himself, had they known of the dark Art Odin had called upon to make him what he was today. But then again, maybe that put Starkad in a unique position to truly under-stand the depths of the horrors sorcery invited. He had touched that darkness himself, had felt its clammy grasp around his throat, and had no desire to feel it once more.

And yet, ever since Wudga had awakened the latent Sight within Starkad, he could never quite shut out the Otherworlds. Visions and dreams melded with uncanny insights and fey intuitions, and the occasional prodding from Odin. Of course, the nightmares had grown even more real in the past moon or so, leaving Starkad to wonder if the sorcerer-king was offering him a subtle reminder of his oath.

No ... Starkad did not fancy owing a debt to Gylfi.

The sight of the sorcerer-king's hall thus brought with it the edge of relief. The knowledge that at least one burden might soon be lifted.

One of Gylfi's thegns welcomed them into the hall and bade them sit and eat whilst the king entertained a foreign dignitary. The thegn led Starkad and Hervor to a long table. Soon a slave brought out venison and carrots and fresh berries—better than they had eaten since leaving Godmund's keep in Jotunheim.

Gylfi himself sat on his throne, shrouded in shadows and barely visible, as ever seemed his wont. Perhaps the darkness suited those who delved into the Art, but Starkad would not have put it past Gylfi to have cultivated such a reputation with care and intention. Half a sorcerer's power probably came from the mystery and awe they surrounded themselves with and the terror they evoked in other men.

The guest the thegn had mentioned stood before the throne, arrayed in traveling clothes rather than the pompous finery Starkad would have expected from a so-called dignitary. The man had to have been pushing forty winters based on the hints of gray in his otherwise blond hair.

"Where's he from?" Hervor asked a shieldmaiden across from her.

"Kvenland."

"Come to talk peace or trade?"

"Peace, he claims. Says his people want us to halt any further raids into Kvenland."

Hervor grunted. "And has Gylfi *been* raiding there?"

The shieldmaiden snorted. "Gylfi doesn't order many raids these days."

Discounting sending the expedition to Thule, of course. The cursed island had taken a great many lives. Men Starkad had called friends. Still, it had given him Hervor.

"So," Hervor said. "The Kvenlanders want Gylfi to influence the other kings of Sviarland, then. Interesting tactic."

Starkad focused on the dignitary, but it was hard to catch his words to Gylfi over the commotion in the hall, what with men boasting and drinking, and some pair of warriors wrestling on the far side the room.

"Word comes to us you are quite the singer," Gylfi said. "Will you grace us with some music?"

The dignitary swept an elegant bow and turned about, taking in the whole hall. He caught the eye of many, seeming to will them to silence. One by one, the men fell still, save for the wrestling match.

When the man at last began to sing, Starkad started. His voice was crisp and clean and somehow brought to mind the image of mountain winds sweeping down over the plains and rustling leaves and grass.

Starkad shuddered, more moved than the cared to admit.

When the Kvenlander sang, time seemed to fold backward, as if this man too had a hint of the Otherworlds about him.

The singer praised the Old Kingdoms and lamented their fall, but too, blamed them for their arrogance. In trying to bulwark the realms of men against the chaos beyond, they tempted fate by calling upon the very powers they feared.

And the result was known to all.

> And in the twilight
> Even the Lofdar's flame did dwindle
> And sacred works came undone
> What was wrought faltered
> And save but ash remained naught

Yes ... The Old Kingdoms destroyed one another, leaving behind naught but ruins and legends. That and a legacy of horrors spread across the world, waiting and deathless.

As the song finished, men and women, thegns and housecarls and warriors and slaves—all stared in shocked awe at the Kvenlander, as if bespelled, their voices stolen away.

"Astonishing talent," Gylfi said at last. "You have a gift, song-crafter. Please, I bid you remain with us a moon or so, share your stories and your songs and partake of my hospitality. I will send messages to my fellow kings and pass on your overtures of peace."

The man bowed again and offered up a crooked smile, as if he'd well known what result his song would have. Then he took a seat at another table and began to drink as though he were any other guest of the hall.

Starkad shook himself, then rose and trod forward to meet Gylfi. The king beckoned him forward until he stood but a few feet from the throne.

"You were long away, Eightarms," Gylfi said, his voice

seeming raspy after the soaring notes the Kvenlander had hit.

"In Jotunheim."

Gylfi frowned and leaned forward into the light, ever so slightly. "I would much like to hear tale of your exploits there." Meaning information on potential threats beyond the Midgard Wall, no doubt. Starkad could little trust Gylfi —besides delving the Art, he was a pawn of Odin—and yet, he had to believe him a lesser threat than the jotunnar.

"Perhaps another time, then. For now ..." Starkad unslung the strap from his shoulder and presented the runeblade he'd taken from Glaesisvellir. "I give you Skof- nung, runeblade of the Skjöldungar. Last wielded by Prince Seskef, an age ago." Or more recently if one counted the flame wraith Starkad had fought.

The king's hand trembled—almost imperceptible, but Starkad had caught it—as he reached for the sheathed weapon. He grasped it, one hand on the hilt, one on the scabbard. With reverent slowness, he drew the blade enough to inspect the runes running down the length of it. "You never cease to amaze, Eightarms."

Starkad folded his arms over his chest and stared hard at the king.

"Ah. Of course. I hold your oath fulfilled, my friend."

Starkad nodded. They would never be friends. Starkad wasn't sure if any sorcerer could ever hold true friendship in the way normal men did. They lost something of themselves every time they used the Art, so he'd heard it said. "If there is naught else ..."

The old man grunted and drove Skofnung back into its sheath. He leaned back on his throne and rested the runeblade beside it. "I fear there is. Much has changed since you were away—some ill and some, I think, of special concern to your companion."

Starkad followed Gylfi's gaze to Hervor.

"What happened?"

"Be wary, Eightarms. A darkness has taken root in Ostergotland. It obscures my Sight and robs my dreams of meaning. And it is spreading."

"Spare me your riddles," Starkad snapped. "Has aught befallen Hervor's family?"

"I fear it has."

❦

HERVOR PACED around the room Gylfi had lent them, casting furious glances at Starkad every time she turned. He could not well blame her for such fury, though it was not like to help the situation much.

"The tales say Bjalmar attacked Hrethel's villages even after a peace was settled. That he betrayed his lord's oath of allegiance and started a fresh war."

"Troll shit."

Starkad frowned. True enough, it seemed unlike the old man he'd met to start a war much less break an oath once given. "Numerous accounts seem to agree with the tale."

Hervor faltered a moment, looking almost queasy.

"What is it?"

She shook her head. Always refusing to share her burdens. "I ... I need your help."

"You hardly need ask for it."

"Good. Hrethel will pay *dearly* for his betrayal. I will carve the lungs right out of his back myself!"

Starkad raised his hands to calm her. "Peace, Hervor."

"Peace! Our former friend imprisoned my grandfather!"

"Be that as it may ... He acted thus because Bjalmar betrayed him first."

"My grandfather wouldn't betray a fucking troll! You think he turned on a man he'd sworn an oath to and started murdering villagers? Out of what? Boredom?"

Starkad reached for her shoulders, but she swatted his hands away. So instead he glowered. "You say Bjalmar would not have done this? If it is so, we must first speak with him and Hrethel both, and learn the truth. You will do your grandfather no favors by rushing in blade in hand. You think they'd let Bjalmar live if you dared attack the king? Your kin would be the first to die."

She blanched, as if suddenly realizing more than pride lay at stake.

"The two of us are not equipped to take on an army, and your runeblade changes naught about that. So, we will go to Ostergotland, call upon Hrethel, and demand answers for his actions."

"His actions are the grossest of betrayals."

Maybe. But Hrethel had fought beside them against Jorund—or against the forces of Prince Rathwith, at least. Without Hrethel, maybe all of Sviarland might lay under the control of Svartalfheim by now.

And Starkad did not fancy casting aside that alliance unless no other option remained to them. Still, he could scarcely dare to hope *any* explanation would suffice for Hervor, given what the king had done to her kin.

3

Starkad lay in almost total darkness.

A terrible crushing weight pressed down upon his chest, driving out his breath and threatening to cave in his ribs. He tried to throw it off him, but could not move. His arms lay limp at his sides. His legs felt pinned by the same weight pressing upon his chest.

Naught but shadows played before Starkad's eyes. An unlit candle sat beside his bed, he knew, but he could not reach it. And against all wisdom, the fire-pit had dwindled down to tiny embers, offering scant illumination.

He opened his mouth to cry out, but no words came. No breath escaped him. Nor could he draw one in, so great became the pressure weighting him down. His ribs were cracking under it.

He felt them warping, straining to maintain their shape as a veritable mountain caved them inward.

His heart had begun to beat out of control.

He tried to call out for anyone who might come, but still had no breath.

A form brushed over his shoulders, and drew up, soft

against his cheek, the contrast against the killing weight on his chest all too stark. A slight exhalation tickled his ear, as if some enormous creature sat upon him, had leaned down over him.

A twisted lover, whispering close to his face.

But the words that came were no language he knew. Harsh and guttural, and seeming to rend his mind and tear straight down into his soul with each syllable that passed the lips of his assailant.

A stream of endless obscenities cutting through his brain and leaving him more and more abject with each utterance.

He thrashed against the alien presence—or tried—but found himself still held tight.

Deep in the shadows, something scurried around him, offering Starkad the tiniest of cruel glimpses at a dark silhouette: some mockery of human form.

This was a dream.

The realization brought with it only momentary relief. This was a dream ... but he wasn't waking up. Why hadn't he woken up yet?

You're not real.

The words wouldn't come from his mouth and thus fell powerless. Or perhaps because, given how the Eitr had changed him, this just might *be* real. A glimpse beyond, into realities man was not prepared to see.

Disembodied fingers began tracing long lines up his shins. They drew higher, up along his thighs.

No. Stop.

An unseen hand cupped around his stones and began massaging them.

He squirmed trying to dislodge whatever held him down. Bile rose in his throat, but he couldn't even retch.

Despite himself, his body responded to the touch, growing hard.

More guttural, alien words whispered in his ear, this time sounding somehow both pleased and threatening. Promising what was to come.

No.

But he knew.

How had he forgotten this? How many times had this thing come for him of late?

Hands were all over his chest, his face, his legs. A shadowy visage leaned over him, a bare hint of a woman's shape.

More hands yanked off his trousers.

A sloppy, overlong tongue lathered over his face, forcing him to close his eyes. He turned his head in disgust and the vaettr licked him. Its tongue grew longer and more bulbous as it trailed down his neck and over his chest.

Stop.

The shadow tongue traced slow circles over the muscles of his abdomen. Then it went lower, lathering around his cock.

Revulsion and excitement suddenly waged war in him.

A hot mouth closed around him. He grimaced, desperately trying not to enjoy the experience.

It wanted him to like it. And to hate himself for liking it. It lusted for his shame more than his body.

He could feel that.

The shadow mouth released him. Offered him a bare moment's respite.

Almost enough to let him think he might escape this time ...

And then it straddled him, drawing his cock inside itself. Thrusting its pelvis back and forth.

Toward the inevitable end. There was no resisting. Not really.

Until he climaxed.

He could almost feel it, sucking tiny bits of his life out, feasting upon the fringes of his soul with each time it took him. Even as merciful oblivion sucked him back down.

4

*L*ong days trekking cross-country did not use to leave Starkad so fatigued. He wasn't sleeping well. The nightmares had been his companions long years now, but they seemed to have changed of late, though the details eluded him. Every time he woke to but a vague sense of unease, of having wandered in some feverish delusion.

And every day he felt a little weaker than the last.

He'd dared to hope handing over the runeblade to Gylfi would abate his torment. It had made not the least bit of difference.

Hervor, for her part, seemed so intent on reaching Lake Vättern and Hrethel's hall there, she had given over any further attempt to interrogate him. Just as well. He couldn't have answered her questions if he'd wanted to.

And he truly did not. As though, were he to but speak of the nameless dread waiting behind his eyelids, it might become more real.

Such was the cost to pay for his long life, perhaps. Or the price of his crimes.

A chill sweat left his neck and beard sticky as they reached the newly constructed town. In the space of less than a year, it had grown substantially, though Hrethel's hall yet dominated the lakeshore. No longer a mere jarl, Hrethel seemed well intent to assert his status to any who came to look upon his overlarge estate. Some might have thought it arrogance, but Starkad could see a kind of wisdom in it.

Those who looked strong were less like to need to rely on blades.

Warriors met them outside Hrethel's hall, and the largest of them strode forward. "Eightarms. He said you might come back here. Can't say as I much believed it."

Starkad stared the man down. That he was known by sight shouldn't have much surprised him. This man? Starkad had no idea who he was. Nor did he much care. "We're here to see King Hrethel."

Some of the other warriors behind the big one shifted nervously. A few fingers twitched. Hands edging toward weapons, though no one drew. Not yet.

Starkad narrowed his eyes at those reaching for blades.

The big man glanced back at the others and gave a single shake of his head. Man had some brains, then. At least one good sign. Maybe they could get out of this without—

"Stand aside," Hervor practically growled at the warriors.

The big man sneered at her. "You must be that shield-maiden who used to follow Haki around. We heard about you too. You want to see the king?" He shrugged. "Be it on your heads." He looked at Starkad. "Best keep the bitch in check, though."

Starkad took another step toward him. "You heard about the expedition to Thule?"

"What of it?"

"She was there. Fought by my side. One of the last survivors ..." He glanced back at Hervor who, predictably, already had a hand on Tyrfing's hilt. "Best keep your *tongue* in check, lest you find out just how good she is with a sword."

The man quirked a smile, but it was clearly forced, and the edge of doubt played in his eyes. "Come on, then. See the king if you will."

The warrior led them into the hall. The throne room was rimmed by a balcony above, allowing a vast gathering to look upon the court. At present, however, no onlookers and but a few warriors gathered here, lounging about and gossiping. Too late for the day meal, too early for the night meal.

The lack of an audience might make it easier to—

"Why in Hel's frozen arse did you betray my family?" Hervor stomped her way toward the king with such fervor that a couple of men jumped up and brandished axes to bar her way. "Who the fuck do you think you are?"

Right. So much for diplomacy.

Starkad strode up beside where Hervor had stopped and leveled his gaze on Hrethel. Come what may, the man *had* acted against Hervor's family. And Starkad had sworn to stay by her side no matter what urd threw at them. If that meant he had to turn on Hrethel ... Well, that would prove unfortunate.

The king rose from his throne and paced forward, then guided away his guards with both hands. "Bjalmar pillaged and razed villages in my lands. Unprovoked. It is out of consideration for *you* that he yet lives at *all*! By all rights, I ought to have hung him from a tree up on the hill and left his corpse to feed the ravens."

"That he lives is the reason *you* yet live, *king*." Hervor fairly spat the last word at Hrethel. "And Grandfather does naught, unprovoked. If he attacked your villages, he had a damned good reason for doing so, I can assure you."

At this rate, Starkad and Hervor would wind up sharing a room with old Bjalmar. Starkad put a hand on her shoulder and pulled Hervor away from Hrethel, just enough to allow him to step forward and face the king. "We have been through rather a lot, the three of us. You hold that throne because of battles I and Hervor helped win for you."

Hrethel waved a dismissive hand. "Perhaps. But there were a great many battles you chose not to take part in, I recall."

"Because we were compelled to uphold an oath to Gylfi. Would you begrudge us that?"

"I begrudge you naught, Eightarms." He glanced at Hervor. "I am a king and yet I have not struck down this woman for speaking to me thus in my own hall. Consider that loyalty. I have not forgotten our battles together. Have you?"

Hervor took another step forward. "You son of a—"

"No one has forgotten!" Starkad bellowed. "Which is why I ask you to release the old man. You cannot intend to keep him here forever. And if you meant him to die, he would have died already. So now we come to you, in peace, and ask for your mercy. Let Bjalmar go and we'll take him away."

Hrethel paced back to his throne now, head in his hand. He did not sit. Just paused there before finally turning around to stare first at Starkad, then at Hervor. "I cannot simply pardon a man who murdered so many people. His shame does not bring back the fallen."

Starkad shook his head. "No, but neither does holding

him prisoner. Naught we do or don't do brings back the dead. And if you do not mean to kill him in vengeance for them, we come back to it—you cannot hold him forever. Suppose though, that I vouch for the jarl and for his conduct henceforth."

"He is no jarl."

Hervor bristled, but Starkad waved her to silence. "Suppose I vouch for him."

After a moment, Hrethel narrowed his eyes and raised a finger. "I will have an oath from each of you. One day, when I call upon you, you will do a service for me."

Hervor sneered. "What service?"

"I suppose that depends on what is needful at the time, now doesn't it? Rest assured, a king oft has need of those good with swords." Now, Hrethel did settle back into his throne. "So what shall it be? Give your oaths and leave with the old man, or not?"

Starkad scratched at his sweaty beard. He had only just fulfilled his oath to Gylfi. Now he was going to get caught up in service to another king. This time, for an unnamed, undecided favor. Funny. Tyr had once told him that Idunn had asked something similar from Odin some three decades ago. A promise that had started the Ás king down a road from which he'd found no return.

Favors.

Messy things.

Starkad straightened, head high. "Very well, Hrethel. I give you my oath. Call upon me, and I will come to your aid."

Hervor glanced from him back to the king. "So be it. I give my oath. Take me to Grandfather."

The king let his gaze linger on the both of them a

moment longer. Finally, he sighed and waved to the big warrior who'd brought them in. "Yes, yes. Take them to see the old man. It's time he was gone from here anyway."

5

*H*rethel's thegn—the big oaf—led them to the back of the hall, behind the king's throne room. There he took up position beside an oaken door and stared a challenge at Hervor. Tempting ... Starkad had already put him in his place, but Hervor's fingers twitched to cut him down to size. Tyrfing practically sung for his blood.

Instead, she threw open the door. The room—a cell—had only a single window, and that a tiny shaft in the upper reaches. Through this a beam of light fell upon her grandfather. Withered and sickly and thinner than Hervor had ever seen him.

His hair and beard had become a gray, tangled mess, and he wore naught but ratty trousers so threadbare they left both knees exposed. His skin had turned almost yellow, a color that had even touched the whites of his eyes.

Driving down the moment's hesitation the shock had given her, Hervor strode to his side and knelt down beside him. Hand on his forehead. "Grandfather?"

He looked up at her weakly. Rasped something she couldn't quite catch.

Fucking Hrethel. That bastard had reduced her proud and noble grandfather from a mighty jarl to a beggar lying in a gutter. He stank from his own piss and shit and who knew how many moons without bathing.

Hervor grit her teeth and rose, hand on Tyrfing's hilt as she stormed back toward that big trollfucker just outside the cell. They knew what they were doing to him. They *knew* he could've died from this treatment.

Starkad interposed himself between her and the thegn before she'd made it out the door. "Stay calm."

"We passed calm a ways ago. *Move.*"

"Hrethel has already agreed to release him. You won't gain aught from starting—"

"I am not the one who started this!"

"Hervor!" Starkad shoved her back into the cell.

Her grip on Tyrfing only tightened, and she bared her teeth at him. If Starkad thought he would stand in her way, he had another think coming. She'd return Grandfather's suffering on these bastards tenfold before she was done. To emphasize her point, she began edging the blade free from its sheath over her shoulder.

Behind Starkad, the thegn's eyes widened as he must have caught sight of the runes lining the blade. Yes ... let him look into the face of Hel. Let him despair, knowing death's gaze lingered upon him.

"H-hervor ..." Her grandfather's rasp stilled her hand, and she turned back to him. "Please ... let this ... be. Let us ... leave."

Hervor looked from her grandfather back to Starkad, then to the thegn. *Someone* had to pay for what had happened here. Such a wrong could be made right only with blood.

"Listen to Bjalmar," Starkad said, hands up in warding. "This path will not avail you, and even less him."

"Some crimes cannot be borne, no matter the cost of vengeance."

"The cost may well be your life, and certainly his. Maybe mine ..."

Oh, bastard. Hold that over her head, would he? She hadn't asked him to do aught here, though he surely should have, given what they had together. He ought to have had his blades in hands the moment he laid eyes on the wreck of her grandfather.

Before she could decide, a pair of men stormed into the cell and grabbed Starkad. A swift twist and Starkad shoved one off—flinging him against the wall—and bore the other to the ground. The guard flailed, caught Starkad's beard and yanked on it.

With a bellow of pain, Starkad slammed a fist into the guard's face. The man fell backward, strands of Starkad's hair tangled around his fingers. The big thegn charged forward, slammed shoulder-first into Starkad, and sent him flying into the wall beside the other guard.

Odin's balls, she wanted to draw Tyrfing! But she'd be forced to kill ...

Instead, she unshouldered the still sheathed blade and raced in. She slapped the big man across the face with the flat. Blood splattered, and the oaf fell, clutching his shattered nose. Hervor twisted and brought the flat down against the back of his skull, sending him sprawling.

The other two guards had risen to their feet, but then, so had Starkad.

"Hrethel gave his permission," Starkad said. "Be somewhere else."

The two remaining men exchanged a glance, and then

the one who'd wrestled with Starkad turned and ducked out the door. The other cursed under his breath. Hervor closed in, sneering at him. If he needed a bit more encouragement ...

But the man finally decided it best to remove himself and disappeared out after his companion.

"Could've gone better," Starkad mumbled.

"Yeah. We could've cut out their lungs and hung their corpses outside Hrethel's walls."

He spun on her. "You need to think this through. Focus on helping your grandfather while he yet draws breath. Lest your temper and need to avenge this wind up costing you all you have left."

She barely restrained the urge to spit at his feet. Fuck him. Fuck him twice—once for being more right than he knew. She *had* pursued vengeance blindly against Orvar-Oddr, and look where that had got her ... Halfway to the gates of Hel and no clue how to find her way back.

And if she let vengeance consume her here ... Yes, she'd make more enemies.

Still, Hrethel would answer for this one day, one way or another. She'd take an oath on that if needs be.

Finally, she looked back at her grandfather, at where he struggled to rise. She slipped Tyrfing's strap back over her shoulder and moved to help him up. Starkad took up his other arm, and together they helped him limp toward freedom.

They'd made it a scant dozen steps when Starkad's legs faltered. "Whoa ..." He swayed for a bare instant, then collapsed onto the floor.

Hervor's grandfather pitched sideways and almost fell over, saved only by Hervor grabbing him.

Odin's balls. Hervor eased Grandfather down to the floor

and knelt beside Starkad. She placed a hand upon his head. He felt feverish and a sheen of sweat built on his brow. "Starkad?" She shook him. "Starkad!"

What in Hel's frozen underworld? He had perhaps seemed a bit off on the trek here, perhaps filled with less vigor than was his wont. He certainly hadn't seemed on the verge of utter collapse.

She shook him again. No, no. This was not good. They had to get out of here before Hrethel changed his mind. They were not among friends in this place.

As she glanced up, the hint of movement in the shadows caught her eye, a figure stepping away from them and into darkness.

Growling, Hervor rose and raced after the figure. She dashed around the corner only to catch a glimpse of someone slipping into an adjacent room. Someone poisoned Starkad? If so, she would wring an antidote out of them.

She jerked Tyrfing free of its sheath. Immediately, the blade began to gleam with a fell fire. She charged into the other room to find a tattooed man sitting in a circle of runes that looked painted in blood. Rimming the circle, candles provided the only illumination in the shadowed room. The strange tattoos on the man's face seemed to dance in the candlelight and cast a wicked gleam upon his face.

Hervor glared at him, advanced, Tyrfing raised high. "A sorcerer. I should've known. You will undo whatever you have—"

A blur of motion to her side. She turned, tried to bring Tyrfing to bear. Someone caught her wrist in an iron grip. With one hand, her attacker flung her off her feet and into the wall. The impact sent blinding lights dancing across her eyes and Tyrfing slipped from her grasp, clattering onto the floor.

She hit the ground the same instant as her sword, took a second battering, lay there groaning.

She hadn't even had time to catch her breath when her assailant grabbed her by the throat, hefted her off her feet, and slammed her back into the wall. The man leaned in, revealing his decaying face in the red gleam in his eyes.

Orvar.

Of course he was behind this. He had brought the sorcerer here to further torment her. Maybe he had even somehow tricked Hrethel into betraying her grandfather. With his hand around her throat, she struggled to make sense of it.

What else might he have been up to in the past year?

She wrapped her hand around Orvar's wrist, tugged on it, tried to pry it free from her neck. But he had the strength of the grave. Making no progress, she took a swing at him.

His other hand jerked up with uncanny speed, caught her fist in his palm. Squeezed until she felt her knuckles popping. She tried to scream, but could get no wind in through her nigh crushed throat.

Everything began to dim. Even the candlelight faded away.

Of a sudden, he dropped her, and she sank to her knees. Sucked in painful breaths. Desperate for air. She tried to look up at him but her neck would barely respond.

His knee jerked up and caught her in the mouth, the blow sending her sprawling on the floor. It jerked her head back so hard it took a moment for the pain to register. She gagged on something hard and jagged, coughed and spit out a tooth along with a glob of blood.

Her mouth was full of wool and bitter iron. Any attempt

at speech was a waste, and yet still she tried to form a thought.

The draug's hand snared in her hair and pulled her back up to her knees. And then his blow smacked into her ribs with the force of a charging ram. She tried to double over with the pain but he held her aloft.

Hervor wanted to weep, to beg, to do aught to make him stop. If only she could make her mouth work. He hefted her higher and it felt like her hair would rip out from the roots.

"Poor little Hervor. So weak. So powerless. Do you want it to end? Would you stride gladly toward the gates of Hel? Oh, but not yet. You will lose everything. One by one, I will destroy all you have ever cared for." The draug pulled her up until her face was level with his own. Until she was forced to look into his red, Otherworldly eyes.

And maybe she wanted to beg. But it wasn't in her. She spit a glob of blood in his face.

Orvar snarled and flung her back to the floor.

"Hervor?" Her grandfather's voice called from the doorway.

No. She tried to cry a warning, but all that came out was a moan. No, he couldn't be here. Grandfather!

Before she could so much as rise, Orvar had closed the distance, seized her grandfather, and pulled him into the room. The draug shoved the old man up against the wall and growled at him, the sound as Otherworldly as his visage.

For an agonizing moment, Orvar held Grandfather like that. And she knew. She knew he was going to die. Right in front of her, and she couldn't do aught about it. Couldn't even get off the fucking floor.

And then Orvar dropped her grandfather and the old man slumped down. The draug glanced back at Hervor.

"Oh, far better for you to watch what is already happening. Let him linger in twilight, gasping in pain in his final days. Until at last you bring out the family cudgel and put him out of his misery. How I wish I could see your face on that day. But worry not, I will always be close. Even when you finally enter into the ranks of the damned, I will be there waiting for you. Expect me, dear Hervor."

She hadn't seen the sorcerer arise, but the man now stood beside Orvar, the two of them seeming cloaked in shadows. Both men slipped out the door. The instant they had fled, a breeze with no clear source swept through the chamber and extinguished all the candles.

Left her in the dark.

6

The shadows spread out like waves on the sea, roiling around Starkad and casting his world in a dance of half-light and pitch darkness. They pooled around his feet as he wandered, muffled his footfalls, and dragged at his heels. They swallowed the pitiful glow of his torch like a hungry beast.

Everywhere he turned he remained trapped into utter solitude, in loneliness so profound it stole his breath away. A quiet so deep, it stifled even the crackle of his torch.

And each plodding step forward became more difficult than the last.

Ahead, through the haze of shadow, figures drifted in and out of focus. Starkad grunted silently, struggling to make his way toward them. The chance to see any other soul, to touch another was like water to a parched throat. But the shadows pulled at him, mired to his waist in a bog of them, holding him back and making each step more difficult than the last.

Starkad opened his mouth to shout for the people in the distance. Only a pitiful wheeze escaped his lungs. What was happening? What had happened to his voice? Again he cried out, managing only a puff of frustrated air.

He couldn't reach them. Why couldn't he get to them? Why couldn't they hear him?

Groaning with effort, he trudged forward. Even his arms felt like they were pulling against the current now.

Another silent shout.

But he'd drawn nigh to the figures at last, people milling about as if they could not even see him. Until one turned, looked him in the face.

Vikar.

Starkad's brother stared daggers at him. The man's throat was chafed raw by the ends of a noose still dangling from his neck.

I'm sorry. Forgive me ...

The words would not come. He opened his mouth, shaped them, but his voice was gone.

I didn't mean ... I shouldn't have ...

Naught but wheezing.

Vikar took a shuffling step toward Starkad, hands raised as if he intended to strangle him. To bring Starkad down to share his awful end. Well-deserved justice come for him at long last.

Another accuser passed by his side. He turned, even that motion feeling sluggish and distorted.

Ogn slapped him across the face. The sharp sound rang in his ears, nigh to a cacophony next to the overpowering silence engulfing him. Her beautiful face, once almost aglow, now seemed ashen in death. Eyes empty sunken in her skull.

Behind her, two more men drew nigh. Alrik and Eirik, each equally dead—if not by Starkad's hand, then by his failures. The brothers bared rotten teeth at him, hissing in wordless, formless wrath.

Forgive me ...

And still he could not speak.

He held his free hand up in warding as Vikar's own hands edged closer to Starkad's throat. Please. Let them all forgive him. But not one of his accusers had the least bit of mercy in their eyes. The dead are unable to forgive aught.

If only he could have explained ...

Instead, he turned, fled deeper into the shadows. Made it a bare few steps before he almost blundered into Orvar-Oddr. His skin gray and rotting off. Eyes gleaming red, damned to the same awful urd as the Axe. As all who died upon Thule.

No!

Fuck! He'd tried! He'd tried to protect everyone!

Starkad ducked around Orvar and dashed deeper into the tide of darkness. Now the shadows no longer impeded him. They jerked him along as if caught in an undertow, threatened to pull his feet out from under him, to engulf him and devour him whole.

He dared to glance behind him. The legions of his victims and failures pursued him. Vikar and Ogn, Eirik and Alrik. Orvar. Yngvi and Alf. The Axe. Jorund. Ivar the Loud. Rolf Quicktongue. Bragi Bluefoot. A hundred others and yet he knew them all.

And they knew him. Deeply as lovers, they knew the crimes and darkness of his soul. Their eyes flickered with the knowledge, glowed with it like tiny candles chasing him through the darkness.

The ground beneath him bucked and revolted like a ship's deck in a storm. Starkad stumbled, caught himself, and raced onward.

And then the stone beneath him cracked and burst apart. A rocky hand lurched out of it and snatched at his ankles. Starkad yelled—tried to—and jumped over the grasping hand. Another burst from the ground, followed by another and another.

One snared his right shin.

He jerked his leg, but the grip held him fast, strong as the stone it was made of. Another hand broke free from the earth and grabbed his other leg. Another and another jerked up. They dragged him down into the dirt. He was buried up to his knees and sinking deeper.

Stone hands snared his thighs, his shirt, his belt. Pulling him under.

Fuck!

Starkad beat at them with the torch. One hand lost its grip and sank back into the earth. Two more burst up to take its place.

Rocks crushed him up to his waist.

A hand grabbed his shoulder. Yanked him downward. Pebbles pelted his face. Dirt kicked up into his mouth. He screamed, still unable to make a sound.

Ogn was there, staring at him. Her eyes were murderous pinpoints of light in the darkness. They were all there, watching him face justice after long years. Hundreds of them.

More of the stone hands grabbed him. Snared his beard and his hair. Pulled him deeper. Grit stung his eyes.

Help!

He tried to reach for Ogn, barely able to get his forearm above the rocks. She sneered, unmoving and unmoved.

Starkad tried to scream but couldn't. Dirt and rock covered his face, blinded him. Filled his mouth until he could no longer breathe. Until he was held motionless. His lungs screamed with fire but could not find air.

The weight of the earth crushed in around him.

He'd been buried alive. He jerked his arms about, desperate to dig himself free. No room to move at all. No chance at aught.

This was his end ...

Sinking ever deeper, until the earth held him in its bowels forever.

The dirt suddenly broke and fell away from his face. Starkad gasped, spat out earth and pebbles and sucked down another breath. Stone blocks held his hands and feet, imprisoned him on the ground.

But he could breathe.

Blissful, beautiful air. No matter it was stale here beneath the land. It was glorious. He was alive.

Alive.

And in a cavern. The only light came from tiny flickers of flame in the distance. He couldn't sit up, couldn't get a good look.

Candles, maybe? Torches?

Figures moved about in the shadows cast by those flames, drifting in and out of his view.

He tried to scream, wheezed. Tried again. Forcing the words up felt like pushing against a mountain. "... help ..." A whisper only.

Two of the figures shambled closer. They were hunched over, misshapen and bent in a mockery of human form. Backs so bent their beards nigh brushed the ground. Dvergar.

Starkad snapped his mouth closed. Dvergar helped no one. Not even themselves. All they wanted was others to share their eternal misery.

The nearest one kicked Starkad in the face with an iron boot. The blow sent blinding lights dancing across Starkad's vision. It took a moment before he could even taste the blood in his mouth or feel the teeth rattling around over his tongue. He spit one out. Another. And another. A half dozen of his teeth gone ...

No ...

The other dverg leaned close over Starkad's face and leered at him, the creature's matted, greasy beard dangling into Starkad's mouth and nose. The dverg grabbed him by both sides of his head. Dug meaty, rocky fingers into his temples with enough force it ought to have cracked his skull.

Starkad screamed now, roared in pain from the pressure.

Finally, the vaettr released him and backed away.

Metal scraped over stone in the distance. Starkad blinked. Hard to focus ... eyes not working through the haze of pain.

He could barely lift his head up. Couldn't see what ... oh fuck.

Another dverg was dragging a massive iron maul behind himself.

"... wait ..."

The other two dvergar cackled. "Wait? Wait for what? Hasn't this waited long enough? How many winters would you like?"

"Blood needs blood."

The one with the maul drew up beside him and hefted the hammer high in both hands.

"No ..." Starkad mumbled. "Please."

The dvergar exchanged looks.

"He said *please*," one of them said.

"Asked for it. Polite."

"Can't argue," the one with the maul said. It heaved the hammer up above its head.

Starkad screamed, even before the maul descended. Before it slammed into his shin. Before he heard the gut-wrenching sound of bone being pulverized.

He screamed in agony, in horror. Screamed until his voice went hoarse.

The three dvergar chuckled. The one with the maul had let it fall to the stone floor. Now he stalked around Starkad's legs, dragging the weapon behind. He came up on the other side.

"Best make it even. Might have a limp otherwise."

Starkad whimpered. Tried to beg but had no strength left in his voice.

The dvergar nodded to one another. The hammer-wielder hefted it once more.

Another awful crunch as bone snapped beneath it.

Starkad had thought he had no voice left to scream. He'd been wrong. His wails of agony echoed over the cavern walls. Rang on and on into the distance.

Somewhere, far away, cheering answered. A chorus of whoops and clapping, the dverg's brethren applauding his work.

As the cheering finally ended, the sound of iron creaking reached him. Cart wheels, rolling over the rocky ground. A mine cart, filled with stones and dirt. A pair of carts, in fact, being rolled over by more dvergar.

"Did he like being buried in the dirt?" one of them asked.

"Best find out for sure."

"One way to test ..."

The dvergar all hobbled over to those carts and each grabbed great handfuls of dirt and rock.

Oh gods ... Starkad thrashed, trying to pull himself free of the stone clamps holding his arms in place. The restraints crumbled all of a sudden. He could make it. His legs wouldn't respond in the least, so he flopped over and pulled himself along the ground by his arms. Had to get away.

Just had to stay ahead of them.

Each foot he covered was a rush of torment through his legs. Had to escape ... He yanked himself over rough stone, dragging his useless legs behind himself.

A lump of dirt and stones fell on his back. Starkad tried to shake it off. Another piled up. And another.

The creak of cart wheels sounded as the dvergar rolled one of them closer.

No.

Damn it, no!

He kept pulling himself forward, tearing gashes into his arms and face. Dirt ripping into his mangled legs.

More rocks thrown atop him weighted him down. Piles and piles of them.

He couldn't move.

Great heaping armfuls of dirt fell upon him. Buried him alive once more. Tumbled before his face and cut off all vision.

7

*E*verything hurt. Every bump the rickety cart passed over sent a jolt of pain surging through Hervor's ribs. Her jaw had become a swollen mess of purple bruises. She could eat naught but broth, and even that burned and stung as it passed her bruised throat.

It all hurt, but there was no one else to drive this cart. In the back, Grandfather sat huddled in furs, shivering despite the summer. Beside him, Starkad lay senseless.

No, maybe not senseless.

He tossed in feverish fits. Moaned incomprehensible objections to whatever fell visions plagued him. Given her own experience with the Art, she didn't even want to imagine what went on in his dreams.

Hrethel had been generous enough to give them this cart and the horse to guide it. That, and not much else. The jarl claimed to know naught of either Orvar or the sorcerer. Maybe it was the truth. Hrethel had quite the large hall and probably couldn't keep track of all his guests.

Truth or lies, either way, the king of Ostergotland could do naught to help her. Indeed, she could think of but one man who might. The very last man she ever wanted to ask for help. After what he had put her through the first time ...

But Gylfi alone might understand what had befallen Starkad. Might, if urd were kind, be able to undo the fell work Orvar's sorcerer had wrought.

But then, when had urd ever been kind?

The cart rolled over a root, even that little disturbance drawing a grimace from her.

The day had already grown late as the town drew into view. A great commotion rang out from the marketplace, people shouting and laughing and cheering. Once she reached the market, the source became clear.

Whole place was clogged with twice the number of vendors as usual and three times the patrons, all wearing their finest, and most at least a little drunk from the looks of it.

Sumaraki. Here she was, finally in town for Sumaraki, and still in no position to enjoy it. The summer solstice marked a new year. She could hardly celebrate aught while Starkad lay in torment and Grandfather suffered in declining health.

No, there would be no joy this solstice. Drink, perhaps, but not in revelry.

There was no way she'd be able to navigate the cart through the marketplace, so she went around, and pulled it up before the king's hall. Even more raucous celebration echoed inside Gylfi's home, but a warrior loitering outside came to inspect the cart.

Though he teetered with a shuffling gait, he sobered at the sight of Starkad lying there, and shouted for help. In moments, Starkad and Grandfather both had each been taken to warm beds within Gylfi's hall.

Someone must've sent for the king himself because

when she turned around, Gylfi was hovering just behind her.

Hervor suppressed her jolt of surprise. "Help him." Her words still sounded slurred in her own ears, as distorted as her mouth felt. And raspy from the throttling Orvar had given her.

Gylfi put a hand on her shoulder for a moment, then stepped around her and ushered everyone else out of Starkad's room. Hervor followed him inside and shut the door behind her.

The sorcerer-king trod over to Starkad's bedside, his own slightly unsteady gait the only indication that he too had partaken of the merriment. The king knelt beside Starkad and laid a hand upon his forehead. No doubt still burning up, as the man had been the whole way here.

For a painfully long time, Gylfi said naught. Just sat there, seeming to stare into oblivion. Finally, he rose. When the king drew a knife, Hervor's hand reflexively went to Tyrfing's hilt. But Gylfi merely nicked his own palm, then sheathed the blade. The king drew his index finger along the cut and used the blood to paint a rune upon Starkad's forehead.

With a groan and creaking knees, Gylfi sat once again, legs folded under him. "Stay very still and offer no distraction. Not a sound, shieldmaiden."

Hervor sat down beside him, glad to get off her feet, and certainly not wanting to interfere with the Art in the least. At the best of times, touching the Otherworlds was fraught with peril and sure to unleash horrors. She did not even want to imagine the consequences of Gylfi making a mistake.

Still, as time dragged on, it became hard not to squirm.

How long had Gylfi been staring at him? A quarter hour? Longer?

Of a sudden, the sorcerer-king lurched backwards with a gasp, caught himself on his hands, and scrambled away from Starkad. The old man stumbled to his feet, mumbling under his breath all the while.

"What?" she rasped. "What is it?"

He continued backing away, hands up in warding against both her and Starkad. "I ... I cannot help you. Forgive me."

The sorcerer flung open the door and fled, tottering down the hall.

What in Hel's frozen crotch?

Hervor scrambled to her feet and chased after Gylfi, caught him several strides down the hall, and grabbed him by the shoulders. "What the fuck?" She barely resisted the urge to throttle him. Even grabbing him sent a fresh throbbing through her ribs. "After all Starkad did to get you that runeblade, you're walking away from him?" Her voice hurt from raising it, pathetic as it still sounded.

A blade slid over leather as one of Gylfi's thegns rumbled toward her.

The king held up a hand to forestall his man, then shook himself free from Hervor's grasp.

She let him, fixing first the thegn, then the king himself with a level glare. "I came to you for help."

Gylfi looked to his warrior, then waved the man away. Then he stole a nervous glance at the room where Starkad lay, and beckoned Hervor away from it. She followed him several paces until they stood alone in a corner.

The king heaved a great sigh, shuddering with the breath. "You ... know the story of King Vanlandi?"

Hervor shrugged. She didn't know the name. Nor care at the moment.

"He was an early king in Sviarland, of Upsal. One of the first after the Old Kingdoms fell."

She glanced back toward Starkad's room. "I don't care overmuch for ancient history." Every time she got the least bit involved in it, things turned rather woeful. Her encounters with the ghosts in Glaesisvellir had been far too much education in the days gone for her liking.

"Vanlandi married this beautiful girl out of Kvenland. Wellborn, and wise, so it's told. And for a little while, they were happy. Then he went out raiding and was supposed to come back. But he didn't. He took up with some other woman.

"So the girl waited and waited, and for many winters he didn't return. Finally, she turned to this witch out of Pohjola. And the witch cursed Vanlandi for his crime of abandoning his wife. She called up a mara—a nightmare vaettr and set it upon Vanlandi."

Hervor frowned. "And you're saying one of these maras is in Starkad?"

Gylfi motioned for her to lower her voice. "Vanlandi complained of nightmares. For days he complained to his people. He felt like something was crushing him in his sleep. He couldn't move, couldn't rest. Woke up more and more drained with each passing night." Gylfi cleared his throat. "And then he died in his sleep. They said his face was a mask of the most stark terror anyone had ever beheld."

Oh, Odin's thrice-damned balls. "Get it. Out of him."

"An exorcism of that magnitude is far beyond my Art. Such an entity ... I dare not even attempt it. Doing so would expose me to its power, as well."

Now she took a step toward him until her nose was practically brushing up against his. "You must try."

Gylfi's eyes narrowed. "Do not take me for one of your drinking companions to be browbeaten or threatened, least of in my own home, shieldmaiden."

Hervor became suddenly aware she was dangerously close to a man who wielded powers she dared not even imagine. But ... Starkad. She wasn't going to let Vanlandi's urd become Starkad's. It would not stand. "If you cannot do it, tell me who can."

Gylfi pushed her away. Not roughly, but clearly at the end of his patience. "Odin, perhaps, were he here. I do not know of any mortal sorcerer that would dare to invoke such powers."

Hervor bared her teeth and shook her head. "Odin? So be it. If I have to track down the Ás himself and force him to help, I will. But this I swear—I will save Starkad."

"You are quick to make oaths, shieldmaiden. Take care that your rash words do not lead you down paths from which you cannot return."

Hervor flinched. Gylfi might have been more right than he knew. But none of that mattered. Not while Starkad lay possessed, maybe dying. They had sworn to stay by each other's sides. They had said ...

No. She would not lose him. No matter what, she would not allow it to happen.

"I need you to get messages to my allies. Send word to any who might come to Starkad's aid."

The old king pursed his lips and nodded slowly.

8

*S*tarkad lay buried in the earth, slowly sinking deeper and deeper. As the hours passed, became days, the land pulled him so far under he would never again see light or air. It wrapped him in a prison of endless pain and crushing weight, holding him motionless.

The ache in his legs had become so constant, he could almost forget it. For a moment or two, here and there.

He couldn't have even said when the mud and rock engulfing him began to grow warm. Had it always been this hot? It must have started slowly, but now he was caked in sweat that had nowhere to go. It lingered, sticky on his skin.

The rock pressed him so tight he couldn't hope to pull away from its scalding heat. He could hear his skin blistering. The only sound really, besides his own whimpers of torment.

The flesh on his arm popped and hot blood oozed out, seeping through the tiny spaces between rocks. It was like a smoldering bog, sucking him ever deeper.

And then his heel was free, hanging in the air. A heartbeat later, his arse was loose. And then he fell, pitched tumbling through scorching hot air for dozens of feet.

He landed in a raging fire, the impact knocking him senseless for a bare instant.

Then screaming. He flailed and tried to throw himself free. His legs barely responded. Flames ignited his hair and beard, his clothes. Blackened his flesh as he crawled from the bonfire. His charred skin ripped apart, oozing, even as he pulled himself clear of the blaze.

He rolled over and lay on his back, gasping.

Why couldn't he die?

Was this ... Odin's fault? Was this Starkad's curse? An extended youth ... followed by never-ending torment?

Smoke burned his lungs, choked him. He coughed, spewing up sickening ash-colored blood and mucus from some ruptured organ. The flames had scalded his eyes, and it stung to even open them.

Still, he forced himself to do it. He lay on his back, staring up at a cavernous ceiling that itself smoldered and glowed incandescent. Ash filled the air, bits of it drifting on a scorching wind that swept around the cavern.

Groaning in pain, he rolled over onto his side. Rivers of magma cut deltas through a broken caldera. In the distance, volcanoes fed those rivers, weeping continuing streams of lava. Beyond, barely visible through the smoke and ash clogging the sky, a lake of fire bubbled. Iron chains with links as big around as a house spanned the enormous gulfs between jutting, spike-covered obelisks.

Trembling at the sight of it all, Starkad turned over and pushed himself up on his hands. The earth itself was searing, sending fresh agony through his already scorched palms.

Just one more stone on the mountain of pain crushing him. He should be dead a dozen times over.

He longed for death.

The land rumbled with an earthquake, trembling like an enraged behemoth. Somewhere ahead, a volcanic geyser vented, spewing sulfur and fresh ash over the hateful landscape.

When the tremors subsided, Starkad managed to gain his feet. Hadn't something happened to his legs? It was hard to think through the haze of torment ... When he tried to walk, new pains lanced up his shins and sent him toppling back to the ground.

"Hel," he grunted.

From within the smoke, something answered, its voice a hideous growl, its words alien and dark. The mere sound of them almost enough to break him.

He struggled to his feet once more, teeth grit against the pain, hands raised up before him. "Where are you ...?"

A silhouette passed through the smoke and was gone, followed by another rumbling growl of torturous words. For a bare instant he thought he saw the pinpricks of glowing red eyes, too large to belong to aught human. Then they were gone.

Fuck this.

Unarmed and wounded, he was in no shape to fight a vaettr of any kind, least of all some flame spirit. Gasping with the effort, he shuffled away from the smoke column he'd seen the figure in. His shambling, lopsided gait carried him with all the speed and grace of a three-legged turtle, but he had to try.

A sulfuric geyser erupted a few feet in front of him, nigh bowling him over with noxious fumes. Starkad threw his arm up in front of his face and doubled back, seeking a way around.

From the column of smoke ahead, another silhouette passed.

Bastards were stalking him.

Grunting, he shambled on in another direction. Just had to get clear. Wherever this abhorrent place was—and part of him feared he knew—he had to get away from the creature.

The smoke billowed around him, encircling him in a flowing black cloud. It forced him to change directions once again. Until there remained nowhere left to go.

Starkad roared at the flames.

And the silhouette formed up once more, striding toward him. Becoming solid, like a man. A deep-skinned Serklander, perhaps, with a tightly trimmed beard just around his chin and lip. Black haired. Unaffected by the flames or choking smoke swirling around him.

"Starkad ..." The same throaty growl that no human ought to have been able to make.

"Be gone!"

The man smirked, drawing closer, hands spread as if in offering. Within the depths of his eyes, a fire smoldered. His smile drew too wide, exposing sharpened teeth. Flames danced beneath his skin, visible through cracks in his flesh, as though magma flowed through his veins. His skin darkened, turned blue as midnight.

The creature inclined its head and there were goat-like horns rising from its brow.

Starkad backed away a step. The smoke cloud brushed against him. He spun and dashed into it, blinded and not caring. Aught was better than staying with this creature.

A hand fell on his shoulder.

Starkad spun, punching with a lightning-fast hook. A

smoldering hand caught his fist and he screamed as fresh burns spread up his arm. The creature flung him through the air, sent him spinning around sideways.

He slammed back into the ground, toppled over, and came to rest a bare foot from a lava river.

Starkad staggered back to his knees.

A flickering vision of flames and unbearable rage washed over him, leaving him reeling. The Fire vaettr closed the distance in an instant as though he'd disappeared from one spot and reappeared next to Starkad. The creature snared him with one hand on his shoulder, bent him over backward, toward the fiery lake.

Its other hand turned into molten lava, glowing so hot Starkad felt his flesh bubbling even as that hand drew nigh. He flailed, but the creature held him in an iron grip. It drew closer.

"No!"

Its hand moved over his face.

"Stop! Please, stop!"

It formed a fist, save for its thumb sticking out.

"Don't! You can't do this—"

It pressed its magma thumb into Starkad's left eye. He heard the sizzle and pop of the jelly even over the sound of his own screaming. Unbearable, mind-shattering pain exploded through his head.

He should have died again from it.

He was lying on the ashy ground. Couldn't see from one eye … of course not. With trembling hands, he reached up and brushed his fingers over the charred skin around his empty eye-socket. Even the faint touch was like burning acid.

He'd begun screaming again. Didn't know when he'd started.

A vise gripped around his ankle and jerked him forward. He fell back, head slamming against the rocks.

The creature dragged him by his ankle, its smoldering fist blistering and burning away Starkad's skin.

Starkad had no breath left with which to scream. He tried anyway.

Couldn't ... couldn't see what was happening to his left. All peripheral vision ... gone.

The Fire vaettr pulled him through enormous piles of ash. Yanked him over coals.

Starkad shut his remaining eye.

Please Odin ... let him die now. Just let him ... die.

A sudden awful clenching of his gut hit him. And with it, the realization: he couldn't die ... because he must already be dead. He had fallen into one of the underworlds. Into ... Muspelheim. The World of Fire.

The creature that held him hurled him forward, sending him tumbling over the rocky ground once more. Despite himself, Starkad pushed up onto his knees again. If he was forever damned, he'd meet his urd head on. Not whimpering like some craven wretch.

He knelt before a mighty obelisk.

No ... a throne the size of a king's hall, the back of it drenched in shadows. And it was occupied. The creature that sat upon this throne towered over him like a living mountain, smoldering in the darkness. Its eyes were pools of molten hatred glaring down at Starkad. Ram-like horns curled down from its misshapen brow.

When it opened its massive maw, magma dribbled out in place of spittle. The monstrosity uttered something in the same guttural tongue the other had spoken, its voice seeming to leave the whole world trembling.

Surely, he now knelt before a prince of Muspelheim. A lord of Fire.

Teeth grit against the pain, Starkad glared defiance at the creature with his remaining eye. He struggled to his feet, sucking in painful, scorching breaths in the process.

The Fire prince raised its hand. Molten steel chains erupted from columns beside its throne. They shot out like arrows and coiled around Starkad's forearms like serpents. Their heat scorched him down to his bones.

He had no screams left in him. No voice left with which to object.

The chains pulled taut, lifting him off his feet and suspending him two dozen feet in the air, almost high enough to look into the searing eyes of the behemoth on the throne.

Its rumbling laugh washed over him in a fresh wave of heat.

Its gaze promised him an eternity of suffering.

9

*N*ever in her life had Hervor imagined she might *want* to find a sorcerer. A woman would have to be mist-mad twice over to desire an encounter with one who touched the Otherworlds. She'd fought Niflung sorcerers, true enough, and lived to tell of it—if only just. But they, as well as Gylfi, had only proved the folly of dealing with such *creatures*.

And here she was, scouring the town and the nearby hills for any would-be wielder of the Art. She'd met a völva who could do less than naught for Starkad and was more like than not a fraud. Her, and no one else. Sorcerers and witches were blessedly rare and most went their whole lives without laying eyes upon one.

For the best—unless someone you loved depended upon finding a worker of the Art. It was the third day and Starkad grew worse with each passing night. Weaker, more wan. Even he, strong as he was, would not last long.

It left Hervor with a difficult choice. Depart these lands in search of someone to help and thus leave Starkad alone. Or remain here. She led the goat she'd bought out into the woods. In the throes of desperation, she'd turn to routes she would never have considered otherwise.

The most powerful sacrifices were human ones, of course, but she'd try this first. Thus far, neither Odin nor any other Ás had answered her prayers. Maybe this would get their attention.

"Odin!" Her raspy cry sent a flight of birds scattering away from somewhere above her. "Odin! I offer you this sacrifice in my time of need!"

She pulled her knife, then jerked it along the goat's throat. The animal bucked in pain and fear and shock. She grabbed its horns and struggled to hold on, to hold it still while its blood spilled out over the grass. Its thrashes sent jolts of agony into her ribs. The animal bleated, the sound garbled and wheezing.

"Odin, aid me!"

"You deserve no aid, murderous bitch."

Hervor's heart leapt into her throat and she turned, slowly. Odin had come here?

It was not the Ás king who strode past the trees, but Ecgtheow.

She gaped at the big man, struggling to make sense of his words. "Tiny?"

"Don't call me that." He had a hand on the hilt of his sword over his shoulder, had already begun to ease the blade free. Not the runeblade though. Didn't seem to have that anymore.

"What are you doing? You answered my call for help ..."

Ecgtheow growled something unintelligible before answering. "I came at your call, yes. Came to right a wrong your actions have wrought. You brought suffering and blood to your kin and mine. To all Sviarland."

Oh ... troll shit. He knew. "Ecgtheow, please. There are things you don't understand."

He snorted. "That supposed to excuse aught? Will you try to justify the murder of our leader, of a member of our crew? You slew Orvar-Oddr, and for what?"

Hervor spat. "For vengeance. The bastard had it coming." She reached up and grasped Tyrfing's hilt. She sure as Hel's frozen underworld wasn't going to let Tiny kill her now. Not for this.

"Did he? Do you have any idea what he has wrought since then? Your betrayal was enough to cause him to rise from the grave, and that with a singular pursuit. Your favorite one, no less—revenge. Now he's destroying everything around you because of it. Everything you touch turns to death, bitch. Be doing all Sviarland a favor to send you down to Hel." He jerked the blade the rest of the way free. "If it makes you feel better, suppose you can call it vengeance."

Damn it. If he forced her to draw Tyrfing, she'd *have* to kill him. And she needed all the help she could get. "Just wait. Please. Listen to me. Orvar used a sorcerer to curse Starkad, to trap him in some nightmare."

Ecgtheow advanced on her, slow and steady, forcing her to fall back. "You're the nightmare here. Best I help this land wake from you."

"He'll die! Starkad will die of this if we do not find help for him!"

Now the big man faltered, let his sword point drop into the dirt. "Can't say as I'm about to take your word for that."

"If you don't, we lose someone we both call friend. Can you afford to lose any more of those?"

He spat. "Don't suppose I can." He looked about a

moment. "If all you say is true, best you take me to him, then. I need to see him with my own eyes."

"All right. All right … He's in Gylfi's hall."

꿍

Ecgtheow shook Starkad again. The third time had as much effect as the first two. "Wake up!" He slapped him and Hervor cringed. "Wake up, damn it!" He looked back to her. "You tried throwing water on him?"

She rolled her eyes.

Grumbling, Ecgtheow rose from Starkad's bedside, grabbed Hervor by the elbow, and dragged her out of the room. "This still falls on your shoulders. Your actions wrought this, no mistake. Can't just let that lie."

"Spare me the sanctimony, Tiny. I am hardly the only warrior in this hall who cut down her enemies."

"That's a fact. But far as I can tell, you're the only one responsible for a draug come back keen on sowing chaos and slaughter across the whole of Sviarland."

Hervor glared at him.

Before she could think of a response, someone approached from down the hall. It took her a moment to recognize the singer from Kvenland she'd seen in Gylfi's hall almost a moon ago.

He nodded to her, and she fell silent to let him pass. Except he didn't. Instead, the man drew up beside her and stopped, stared right at her.

"Can I help you?"

"How magnanimous when the one seeking aid begins by offering it. Word spreads you find yourself in a dire plight and now called for anyone learned in the Art, heedless of the danger or implications therein."

Hervor balked, but it was Ecgtheow who spoke. "Who the fuck are you and what are you on about?"

"An emissary of Kvenland. Väinämöinen is my name, and having traveled far and long, a great many secrets have unfolded themselves before me. Arcane knowledge that might prove somewhat fortuitous under the circumstances."

Hervor shook herself. If the man was here to answer her prayers, who was she to complain? Maybe Odin really was listening. "You can exorcise a vaettr?"

Väinämöinen stepped gingerly around her and strode into Starkad's chamber. There he examined her lover.

Ecgtheow shoved her back into the room and she stumbled, barely keeping her feet.

She was about to glare at him, but at that moment Väinämöinen turned to her. "A mara has taken root within him, gorging itself upon the dwindling life."

"That much I already know."

The Kvenlander nodded as if to himself. "Yes, and I might be able to exorcise it. Such a ritual is wrought with risk for both him and myself, though. Were I to fail in such a dangerous undertaking, were the vaettr to prove too strong, I might find myself its new vessel." He clucked his tongue. "Difficult and dangerous, a fearful combination to make the most learned of sorcerers tremble."

He spoke almost as if he'd seen Gylfi's exact reaction. Hervor took a step forward. "If this is about money, I'll pay aught in my power to give. But name your price and I'll arrange it, only save Starkad from this vaettr."

"The price of a thing, the woman asks, knowing not the cost he needs."

"If that's a poem, I don't have time—"

Väinämöinen quirked a wry smile. "And if it is but a line from a song that might have been? Time grows short, flitting and flying, before its end. If you wish me to risk so very much, you must risk in turn. In northern reaches, beyond the distant shores from which I hail, you might chance upon the witch-queens of Pohjola. And there, were you to make an end of the one called Loviatar, all would surely hold your payment fulfilled."

Ecgtheow groaned. "Can't say as I much like the idea of traveling to Pohjola."

Nor Hervor. She'd heard stories of it back in her pirating days. Of a land of cold and darkness like unto Niflheim itself, lying north of the kingdoms in Kalevala that made up southern Kvenland. Men said witch-queens ruled there, calling up terrible sorcery to stay young and beautiful.

And here she'd gone and offered him to name his own price. "I meant to say I will come up with gold, with silver, with aught else you desire. I cannot afford a trek to some far-off land." Nor did she relish the idea of going out in the frozen wastes a third godsdamned time.

"Though intent may have been wealful or woeful, still the ends remain the same. For what is needful fades little, but rather flourishes down through time's wretched march."

Ecgtheow scratched his beard. "Uh ... huh?"

Hervor threw up her hands. "Fine. Fine, you want me to hunt down this Loviatar, I'll do it. But first save Starkad. Hel's gate, he'd be the best one to help me accomplish such a murder."

"A payment delivered when the service is far from certain? However pure the intent, failure remains a possibility one cannot deny in such an undertaking."

"A lesser chance of that with Starkad at my side," she snapped.

"And yet here we stand, while he lies wilting in darkness."

Ecgtheow cleared his throat. "Why do you even want this witch-queen dead? What's she to you?"

Hervor spun on him. "I don't give a troll's rocky arse *why*! We don't have time to do this. Starkad will be dead before we could ever reach Kvenland's shores! Much less trek through Pohjola, kill the witch, and get back here."

Väinämöinen's irksome smile only grew, and he drew forth a wooden carving from a pouch. He held it in the palm of his hand, up so she could look closer. A finely carved kestrel, from the look of it. "A soul-bird to soar between the realms of waking and sleeping, to guide the weary soul away from destruction, whilst it wanders in the dark lands."

Hervor frowned at the hunk of wood. "This bird will keep him alive?"

The Kvenlander set the statue down beside Starkad's bed. "All things have their time. I will watch, and stave off the end, so long as I may."

"Meaning we have time, but not much." Bastard.

The man spread his hands. "When the last breath leaves the witch's cursed lips, the wind will whisper of her fall. And hearing its song, I shall begin my own. A verse that might drive our foe from your companion."

Hervor glanced at Ecgtheow and he nodded, albeit with obvious reluctance. "Fine." She looked back to Väinämöinen. "How are we to find Loviatar?"

"Follow the North Star until you can go no further and the world ends at a pillar scraping the sky. The witch abides between this world and the next, in the place where all light dies and fire cannot touch."

So. These witches lived in northern Kvenland. Ilona had come from there, had trained there with witches. What had she called them? Seidkonur? So were these witch-queens the descendants of Ilona's people?

Either way, it mattered little. "We need to be off."

"Oh, indeed," Väinämöinen said. "For all the grace of the soul-bird and all the ministrations I might provide will not avail long. A moon, at most, and then time will have its due."

A single moon?

Hervor didn't spare the strange man another glance.

PART II

First Moon
Year 30, Age of the Aesir

10

*M*ore like than not, Ecgtheow shouldn't have set foot on this ship. Gylaug had gotten word of Hervor's call for help—Ecgtheow didn't suppose he quite wanted to know how Gylfi reached the pirate out at sea— and had shown up in Upsal just when Hervor was off hunting a vessel to ferry them to Kvenland.

Timing was a bit too perfect to Ecgtheow's mind. Such things bespoke of either dark urds, or men meddling with the Art. Or both.

And here he was, heading for unknown lands, and not for any raiding either. No, he could've stayed in Ostergot-land. Ylva had begged him to stay with her, with their newborn son. Except word had reached him about Hervor come calling on Hrethel, and after all she'd wrought, he couldn't rightly just let her be.

So he'd gone to kill her.

And somehow wound up sailing beside her, on the same crew once again with the lying, murderous shieldmaiden.

Such was urd.

A strong wind helped them make good time, too. Could

be natural. Best to hope it was, he supposed. Either way, Gylaug had a cocksure grin on his face as he made his way to where Ecgtheow stood nigh to the bow.

"You seen these lands before?" Ecgtheow asked the pirate captain.

"Kalevala? Sure, I've raided up and down the Mori-marusa and Gandvik, both. Plunder, trade—both can profit a man who knows what he's about." The captain had earned himself a fresh scar over his brow since last Ecgtheow had seen him. That, and a habit of scratching at it so fierce just watching pained Ecgtheow. "Never went to Pohjola, though. Not many a man has, leastwise not many who came back. Kvenlander men, fools and princes—much the same, I guess—sometimes they go up there hunting beautiful brides. Can't say as I've seen too many of these brides, though."

"And we can't sail there?"

Gylaug snorted. "Want to guess how many ships have come back from those waters? Where they're not frozen solid, they're thick with more icebergs than I've got hairs on my arse." Not an image Ecgtheow needed in his brain, but there it was. "Right, even if there weren't for the ice, tales go way back about the spawn of Jormangandr. Serpents fit to swallow a whole longship."

"Huh. So who tells these stories if the ships get swallowed whole?"

Gylaug chuckled. "Don't go doubting the wisdom of men of the sea, my man. You'll wind up caught in Rán's net faster than you can blink."

Ecgtheow looked back from the pirate to Hervor. She hadn't even bothered disguising herself as Hervard this time. Was just standing by the gunwale and staring out over the deep, hand to her ribs. The shieldmaiden had clearly taken a beating not long before he came upon her. Bruises on her jaw seemed mostly faded, but her voice sounded like someone had tried to hang her. Maybe they did—she'd have deserved it, no doubt on that.

"Fancy her, do you?"

Not fucking likely. If he told Gylaug she'd murdered the captain of her own ship, would he throw her to the sharks? Sure as Niflheim was cold, she well deserved that too. That and a thousand torments beyond to go with it. Hervor was a traitor, whatever her reason. But she *was* clearly loyal to Starkad.

Maybe even in love with him.

Ecgtheow didn't suppose that was much his concern, except he happened to like the man, notwithstanding his choice in women. So it didn't much serve Starkad to kill someone trying to save his life. Not now. Still, there had to be a reckoning.

Hervor had stirred up a blizzard of troll shit and half of Sviarland wound up stinking on account of it. It wouldn't hold for her to get to walk away without her fair share of the muck caking her.

"You spent a lot of years as a pirate," Ecgtheow said.

Gylaug snickered. "More than a few. Kind of a family trade, truth be told. Don't think that means I didn't notice you changing the topic to avoid the question."

"What?" Oh. Hervor ... "I don't fancy anyone but my wife. I was just thinking ... you ever have a member of your crew go ... too far?"

"Ugh. You mean what? Can't say as we have all that many rules one has to follow. Just loyalty to your crewmates and to me, mostly."

"And what if someone broke that rule?"

Gylaug shrugged. "What do you think happens to 'em?

73

Don't talk like you're some child still wet from your mother's teat. A man goes too far against his own, his own put him down. It's the way it's always been. Has to be. If you can't trust the men at your back, you're already halfway to the gates of Hel."

Ecgtheow supposed he *was* at that, and from the sound of it, they were sailing closer with each passing hour.

AND BUT A FEW HOURS LATER, Gylaug's ship made port at a small town in Kalevala. To Ecgtheow's eyes, it looked not much unlike a seaside town in Sviarland. At least until they drew up close, and he caught a glimpse of the people.

Mostly blond-haired, and clad in bright reds and blues, vibrant shades that looked like they were arrayed for a festival instead of work. And still, these people set about helping tie off the ship.

They spoke the North tongue with a strange accent, seeming to overemphasize the vowels and draw out their words a bit too long. Still far better than South Realmers, he supposed.

When they were tied off, Gylaug shouted to some of the crew to trade for supplies. "Brandt is in charge while I'm away. I come back, the ship best still be where I left it. Kustaa, Latham, you're with us."

The two men he'd called out joined him at the gang-plank and followed him down onto the docks. Hervor chased after him and Ecgtheow followed, glaring at her back. Leading them all into the gates of Hel, no doubt about that.

Still, he owed Starkad. That meant taking any help he could get to save the man.

At the edge of the town proper, Hervor pulled up short, staring at a man sitting on a crate, just under the eave of a warehouse. Though he looked familiar, Ecgtheow couldn't place him.

"Wudga?" Hervor asked.

Oh. Volund's son. Hel's tits.

Ecgtheow had dared to hope he'd seen the last of Wudga. The svartalf's bastard had nigh gotten them all killed, and even in the end he couldn't say for certain whose side the man was on.

Wudga slid off the crate with the grace of a dancer and quirked one of those annoying smiles men had when they thought they knew more than you did. "You asked for me."

Right. Too much to hope Hervor would've thought better of asking this one for help. Far as Ecgtheow could tell, she just had Gylfi send for anyone she'd ever met. Knowing Hervor, half the people she contacted were probably keen to kill her.

Come to think of it, how did Wudga know they'd be here? In this particular port? Had Gylfi been able to tell them that? None of this sat overwell with Ecgtheow.

Hervor approached Wudga, clasped his arm in her own. Just like they were old friends. Like they had not been at each other's throats a year ago. "I'm glad you came."

"Maybe I owe it to Eightarms. As it is, there's someone you need to meet." Wudga beckoned and led their small crew into the town.

11

*I*n truth, Hervor was loath to trust Volund's son. The man was capricious, unpredictable. And she had more than half a notion he had let Volund go. No surprise really. After all, who could truly strike down their own father?

Still, she had to believe Wudga would come to Starkad's aid in such circumstances. They had been friends a long time, long before what happened with Jorund and the svartalfar. Finding herself in the throes of such desperation, she had to turn to any who might help. And thus, having no alternative, she had related their mission here, struggling to talk, much less to do so without letting on how much pain she was in.

Wudga nodded. "I'd gathered much along these lines from Gylfi. Hence, I procured the help of one better suited to navigate to Pohjola."

"A woodsman?"

Wudga chuckled. "A shaman. Like a male völva, more or less. Pohjola is a land closer to the Otherworlds than our own. A place of darkness, where reality is tenuous and not all is as it seems. The only hope of crossing it will come from one versed in Otherworldly lore."

Odin's balls. Everything she heard about this place made her mislike it all the more.

She cleared her throat, even that causing a fresh twinge of pain. "I met a man from here, back in Dalar. The one who sent me here on this mist-mad quest. As he hails from your own kingdom, what can you tell me of Väinämöinen?"

Wudga cast her the briefest of glances, a hint of a smile upon his face. "What can I tell you? Little but what you must have already garnered. The man is a vagrant, a wanderer. Always seeking."

"Seeking what?"

"Even had I the answer to that, I doubt you would much like to hear it. The pursuits of those steeped in the Art are best left be."

Hervor frowned. It wasn't quite the answer she was looking for. In fact, she wasn't sure it was quite an answer at all. "And how did you find yourself in Kvenland?"

"My father was kin to the king, a relation I called upon to win myself a comfortable abode here. I don't always linger in this town, but it suits me from time to time."

Indeed, he led her to a hall that would've suited most jarls. The place was surrounded by a hefty stone wall with a decorated wooden gate Wudga threw wide. The man stepped inside then beckoned her and the others to follow. He led them up to the house proper, and inside.

A sizable fire pit kept the place plenty warm, comfortable enough that Hervor shrugged off her fur cloak. Though well furnished, the house had almost no decorations and showed scant signs of anyone living there.

Save for the man sitting before the fire. His cheeks and brow bore tattoos not so very unlike those she had seen on the sorcerer with Orvar. The dark circles under his eyes looked almost too deep, as if shadows had pooled there. And the eyes themselves ... They stared at her as if they could see straight down into her soul. All her crimes laid bare.

Hervor cleared her throat, averted her eyes. Shamans and sorcerers. Hel take the lot of them.

"Hervor," Wudga said. "May I present Pakkanen."

The shaman did not rise, though from the corner of her eye, Hervor caught him incline his head. "The shieldmaiden who would dare to trek across Pohjola."

Now she did stare a challenge at the shaman. Yes, she would go through Pohjola. She would go wherever the fuck she had to in order to save Starkad. "Are you here to help or not?"

"Indeed. You will need more than swords to cross the lands in the north." Now the man did stand. He drifted around the house, pausing before each member of the small crew Hervor had assembled.

Gylaug met his gaze for a moment before looking away. Kustaa and Latham didn't even manage that much. Ecgtheow squirmed under the man's relentless observation, but at least held his own.

Finally, the shaman came back around to her. "I will serve as your guide in the dark lands. You must remain vigilant. You must heed my words. One misstep, and none of us will return from this."

Hervor nodded grimly. No choice remained in the matter. Starkad could afford no delay.

12

*F*or an age, Starkad hung, suspended by molten chains. Until the prince must have tired of the game. For a pit opened beneath him, billowing smoke rising up out of it. The chains grew slack, dropping him into the smoky hole.

He landed on his knees, and his arms dropped limp to his sides, scorched and useless. It felt like they'd been pulled out of their sockets. Like they ought to simply fall off.

The chains melted away.

Dark silhouettes stalked through the shadows. More of the smaller Fire vaettir. More tormentors. But Starkad had no strength left with which to suffer. No hope. And without hope, it became hard to even care about the torment.

One of the creatures strode forward, a smoldering iron in its hand. It jerked the rod forward and branded it against Starkad's chest—his clothes had long since turned to ash. The brand seared his flesh. He was screaming. The sickly-sweet stench of his own cooking skin wafted into his nostrils.

He bucked, flailed, and tried to crawl away.

He'd been wrong. The fresh agony *was* enough to motivate him.

Another of the creatures drove a second brand into his arse cheek. Starkad jerked away, shrieking.

Hideous laughter echoed through the cavernous hole.

How long must this go on? Until the end of time?

A raven cawed in the distance. The Fire vaettir jerked around, suddenly silenced. All but one disappeared back into the smoke. The last stood, turning about slowly, as if seeking the source of the cry.

Another caw.

Starkad froze. The vaettr was looking away. Seeking the bird.

Hope was its own torture.

But then ... even a small chance at freedom was one a prisoner had to take. Stifling his groans, Starkad stumbled out into the smoke. He blundered his way, unable to see much even from his remaining eye. Ash clogged his sinuses and choked him.

His shoulder bumped into a rock wall, sending a fresh jolt of pain into the swollen joint. Trying to keep silent, he followed the wall until it opened up into a tunnel.

Anywhere was better than here ... Starkad stumbled forward, fast as he could, his aching legs not even managing a brisk walk. Had to get faster. Had to move ...

The ground gave way beneath him. He dropped into an angled shaft, banged his head against the roof, and shot downward, tumbling end over end. His shoulder slapped hard on the slope. His bare arse earned a dozen fresh cuts. The whole world spun and pitched and heaved.

And then he was free falling through a half-lit cave. He crashed down into a pool of water, hard, sunk ten feet and hit the bottom. The cool waters stung his open wounds but offered a brief respite from the searing burns. He scrambled upward, burst through the surface, and sucked in a clean breath.

Coughing and sputtering, he swam toward the edge of the pool. His hands slapped against rock and barely managed to pull himself up. To roll over. He lay in a shallow cavern, sunlight piercing in from a wide opening beyond the pool, stinging his eye after so long in the dark.

Finally freed of the tortures, the pains and loss washed over him anew. Every surface of his skin was a scorched ruin. Lances of fire shot through his empty eye socket. His arms and legs felt mangled beyond all repair.

The light ... the open sky.

Despite the pain, Starkad managed to pulled himself along the side of the pool toward the cavern's exit. Had to get out ...

It wasn't a pool. It was a natural spring, slightly bubbling from somewhere deep underground. A glittering stream flowed out of the cavern and down a slope. Starkad had to blink against the brightness outside.

Thick forest grew up in all directions, verdant and almost overpowering. The sunlight shone down through gaps in the thickest canopy he'd ever seen. Not even Vana-heim—Asgard—boasted so dense and varied plant life.

Grunting, he pulled himself alongside the stream's bank, then collapsed there, letting the waters brush up against his cheek, one arm dangling into the stream. It cooled his aching fingers.

Thought seemed to flee from him, offering a reprieve from the anguish that had plagued him for so long he could remember naught else.

He lay there, faint and barely conscious, and grateful for it.

Until the sunlight piercing the canopy turned fiery orange. Within moments, it dimmed completely, and the forest grew drenched in heavy shadows. The branches above actually seemed to stretch, to tangle with each other, obscuring the hints of starlight that might have otherwise offered faint illumination to the forest floor.

Only the stream glittered with slight reflected light.

Starkad pushed himself up on his hands and knees. Stared at the branches overhead. They didn't just seem to be stretching ... they were fucking *growing*. Edging ever tighter. Now he struggled to his feet.

Vines stretched from one tree to the next, forming veritable walls around him. Roots tangled and crept slowly over the opening to the cave he'd come from, denying any attempt to return. All around him, branches and leaves and creepers closed in like a net.

"Shit."

Grunting in pain once again, he waded into the stream —the only place half clear of greenery. The waters rose up almost to his waist, made walking an exercise in frustration.

Roots burst from the land beside the stream. A wall of them grew across the waters themselves, creating an impassible barrier that grew denser and more tangled with each moment.

Starkad cursed under his breath and changed direction, stumbling out of the waters and onto the bank. Only a narrow opening in the underbrush remained, but he could see no other way forward. He shambled for it, twisted his ankle and stumbled into a tree.

Vines wrapped around the trunk broke away and crept toward his wrists.

With a cry, he fell back, caught himself and dashed on into the rapidly closing opening. More vines lurched down from the canopy, grasping at him. Starkad dodged to the side, fleeing, almost blind in the dark wood.

He dared a glance behind him. The forest had closed in, trapped him here. No way left but forward. He blundered ahead, ducking a low hanging branch that seemed to reach for him, and dashed around a pair of writhing trees.

"Get the fuck away from me." His foot caught on another root and he tumbled to the ground.

A tree trunk before him rent in half, oozing discolored sap like pus from a wound. Something pushed against the sap, a face. A female form stepping out, lithe and naked. An ash-wife, her skin gray and almost bark-like.

He struggled to his feet as the creature sauntered toward him, every move accentuated, sensual. Starkad tried to back away, but a cradle of roots and vines rose up behind him and caught him.

The ash-wife reached him and pushed him down by his shoulders. She leaned in, her hair tickling his face. Her warm lips on his. Her tongue pushed into his mouth, its surface slightly rough, its taste heady and rich. Her hands cupped around his cock, massaged it until he was hard as a log. Didn't take long.

And then she was atop him, drawing him inside her. Warm and wet and throbbing, if a little coarse. All other thought fled from him. Dimly, he noticed flowers blooming all around them, an explosion of life. None of that mattered in the least though. All that mattered was the fervor with which the ash-wife pumped her hips. Her hands tangled in his hair. Her tongue licked along his jaw.

Her teeth nibbled on his ear.

She bit down. Hard.

Starkad grunted, gasped, and tried to shove her off. Her bark arms were like iron, holding him down. Her teeth snapped through his earlobe and tore a piece out of it. Hot blood streamed down his neck as he screamed. Her fingers dug into his shoulders like nails into wood. Still she was pumping and grinding, even as his cock tried to wilt from the horrific pain.

Vines from his seat grew up around his elbows and jerked him down. Tightened until they cut off his circulation. More of them crawled all over him. He thrashed, trying to pull free, but was held fast.

Another vine slithered its way up the side of his throat. It pushed over his face. He turned his head aside, trying to break free. The ash-wife grabbed his chin and forced him back, squeezed his jaw until she forced a crack open. The vine kept edging closer. Its tip forced itself between his teeth, wedging into the gap where one was missing.

It started crawling down his throat. Its rough surface ripped at his insides, edging deeper and deeper, cutting off his screams.

Another vine writhed beneath him. It wriggled its way between his arse cheeks and then began to climb up his arse. Starkad thrashed, writhed, bucked. Tried to wail at the gruesome violation. The vines just kept crawling deeper inside him, like they intended to meet in the middle.

Roots dragged him deeper into their grasp until only his face remained exposed.

He knew tears ran from his eyes. He had no care left for shame.

No care for aught, save a desperate, futile prayer.

To die.

13

*T*he straps cut into Ecgtheow's shoulders as he dragged the hunk of bear meat behind him. More like than not, Kustaa was enjoying pulling the other half of the beast almost as much as Ecgtheow was this one.

Hard to say for certain, though, given Kustaa rarely spoke two words, and never in the same sentence. The man's face was a mishmash of scars that made him look like he'd dived head-first into a briar patch. A man with that many scars was either a poor fighter, or a vicious one. Given Kustaa seemed more than alive and had arms the size of a mammoth's legs, Ecgtheow figured the pirate fell into the latter category.

The two of them lagged behind the rest of the crew, heaving and huffing, pulling everyone's night meal along. Wudga had downed the bear—man was always wandering off on his own, but oft came back with a fresh kill—and claimed it only right someone else ought to do the hard work of hauling the carcass. And Kustaa and Ecgtheow were the biggest and strongest, Ecgtheow had to admit.

Didn't make pulling the meat over miles of woodland and roots and hills and such any more appealing.

Forests of evergreens covered the north reaches of Kalevala. Ecgtheow supposed they'd be making way into Pohjola soon enough, not that he expected any clear-marked boundaries. Just that, despite the summer, already they'd felt the bitter winds out of the north. Even caught a few flurries of snow last night. Could hardly call that a good omen, snow in summer.

No, he didn't suppose this journey was going to end well. Time was, he'd have welcomed the adventure. Thule had more than half cleared him of that way of thinking. Dealing with svartalfar and draugar and so forth back in Sviarland had put paid to what little remained of the notion.

Skalds might make some damn fine poems over those who slew creatures from the Otherworlds. Well and good, he supposed, except that those same creatures wound up doing most of the slaying from what he'd seen.

"There's a clearing up ahead," Pakkanen called out. "We should break here for the night." Better words Ecgtheow had never heard, nor was like to again, he supposed. "We may reach Pohjola tomorrow." See—and there was some worse words just waiting for him.

"Guess we can finally put these damn things down," he said to Kustaa.

The scarred pirate looked in his direction. Grunted like a dog. And kept on pulling.

Pretty much his response to everything.

Wudga stepped out from behind a tree, giving Ecgtheow a start. Maybe the man had chosen to remain human instead of going into the dark like his father—Ecgtheow had heard Starkad talk like that. Still, something remained more than a bit unnatural about Wudga. He made no noise when he walked. Like a fucking vaettr, creeping around in the night. Just wasn't right.

"Thought you were more of those wolves for a moment there," Ecgtheow said.

Damn pack had been trailing them the last two miles, at least. Always just out of sight, save for a few glimpses here and there. A few barks, growls. The godsdamned howling.

Wudga shook his head. "These are not the leanest moons. Wolves won't draw over nigh to people unless mad or starving. Had we come this way in the depths of winter ... Well, we might get a closer look at the beasts."

Right. "I've seen more than enough for now, just the same." Besides, in winter, they'd have had dogsleds. Instead of using himself like a damn pack mule.

The clearing, as it turned out, housed the crumbling foundations of what must have once been a watchtower. At its highest part, it now stood no more than a head higher than Ecgtheow himself, so he couldn't judge well how tall it had reached when in use. Broken stones from the tower were scattered around the clearing, some half-embedded in the ground.

Gylaug and Hervor had already started pitching tents while Latham was kindling a much welcome fire.

Ecgtheow dragged the meat over to where the other pirate crouched, shrugged off the straps, and collapsed on the dirt. Cold and hard, true, but just getting off his feet was welcome at the moment. To Ecgtheow's surprise—and delight—Latham had turned out to be more than a decent cook, preparing their meals every night, whenever someone managed to down game.

He was also a better conversationalist than his friend Kustaa. Better by far, Ecgtheow had to admit. He'd carry on enough for the both of them, talking about how he ought to have been a skald and would've been, if he hadn't been so damn good a shot with the bow. From what Ecgtheow had seen, it was only half a boast.

Ecgtheow stretched out his aching legs. "Bear meat tonight, huh?"

"Right you are. And more than a few nights after." Latham tapped the side of his face as if that had been some private joke. "Can't say I've had overmuch chance to cook bear before, but don't you worry. I know a trick or two to make sure any meat comes out succulent enough. Isn't that right, Kustaa!"

Kustaa grunted.

Latham pointed at him. "Right you are. I know my meats."

"I'd make jest of that," Hervor rasped from inside a tent. "Except it just seems too obvious."

Ecgtheow cast a wary glance her way. She'd mostly avoided him on their trek through Kalevala, and he didn't much mind it. Circumstances being what they were, he needed her. Didn't mean he had to like her and sure as Hel's tits didn't mean he'd trust her.

Pakkanen shuffled over and sat beside Ecgtheow, warming his hands by the fire. "In times long ago, this place was built by the Old Kingdoms to watch over the border of Pohjola. Even back then, they knew it for a fell place where men best not tread. Things will grow more perilous from here on out."

"The Old Kingdoms?" Hervor asked, coming over to join them. "You mean by the Lofdar."

Pakkanen cocked his head to the side. "Yes. How did you know?"

Damn good question. Hervor just shook her head, keeping yet more secrets to herself.

Pakkanen shrugged, then folded his legs beneath him, hands resting on his knees. He shut his eyes then, swaying gently back and forth.

"Whoa now," Latham said. "We don't need any of that witchery and black magic going on. I'm cooking here, in case you hadn't noticed."

Pakkanen kept his eyes shut. "Yes. You are cooking *bear*. Therefore we must give thanks to the great bear spirit, and pay our respects for his gift of one of his children."

"Eh ..." Latham wiggled a little. "You're gonna thank someone for letting us eat his children? If that's how you do it around here. Have to be honest though, a man comes to me and thanks me for letting him eat my son, I'd put an arrow in his eye."

"You have a son?" Hervor asked.

"Got two sons and a daughter, as it were. Least, those are the ones I know of, if you follow me."

Hervor snorted. "No. The complexity of your innuendos eludes me."

Latham pointed at her. "Right you are, then. Call it three children, strong and healthy, Odin be praised."

Odin be praised, indeed. The way Ecgtheow saw it, they were like to need the blessing of the gods before long.

"Where's Wudga?" Gylaug asked after a moment, scratching at his brow.

Wudga. Damn bastard had no doubt slunk off into the wilds again, and with the sun already dipping low. It just wasn't natural, a man so comfortable with the night. Fire is life. Stick by the fire. That's what men were meant to do. And Wudga didn't get scared enough. Always popping in and out of the group like he was just as at home in the wilds as he would be in the town.

"Are we sure we can trust him?" Gylaug asked.

Ecgtheow glanced at Hervor. "Hard to be sure who to trust, really. A man can't know what goes on in another's head, can he?"

Latham pointed at him. "That is a fact. We've been fooled before, haven't we Kustaa?"

Kustaa spit into the fire.

Hervor glared back at Ecgtheow. That woman was going to get some or all of these people killed, Ecgtheow supposed. He owed it to his wife and son to make sure he wasn't among the dead.

A task almost as difficult as their mission here.

14

The sound of something pecking on the wood around him woke Starkad. He knew he lay enmeshed in a cocoon of roots and vines. Perhaps he'd remained trapped here an age, his soul slowly rotting away. But the sound and the vibration had woken him. Forced him back to painful, hideous consciousness.

Forced him to re-acknowledge his own damnation.

If he was dead, he could see why the fallen would hate the living. Would hate all that existed. Most of all themselves.

And still, some pathetic, masochistic part of himself wanted to survive.

Desperately, he clawed at the surrounding roots. The pecking continued, rattling inside a skull that roots had long ago rent asunder. He tore at the vines until his cracked fingers caught hold of a root. He grasped it and yanked, finally pulling it free. His hands met dirt.

And kept clawing, forcing his way to freedom.

The roots split and broke apart, and he tumbled out of their fibrous ruins to land on soft dirt. Vines jerked out of his throat and arse and ears, all pulling free with painful rips that shredded his insides from top to bottom.

He lay there, blood and tree sap oozing from nigh to every orifice in his body. Finally, he drew in a breath. The air felt like a hundred knives tearing through his savaged throat. It burned his lungs and set him to a fit of coughing, until he retched, heaving up leaves and dirt and clumps of moss.

And then he collapsed, unable to even open his eyes. Maybe he slept another age—he could not say.

When he opened his eyes, he still lay in a forest, albeit not nigh to so dense as before. The canopy was light, exposing a larger, closer moon than any he'd seen before. It looked so nigh to the land a bird could have flown to it. So large it dominated the sky, blocking out most view of the sky.

A grunting wail escaped him as he pulled himself to his knees. Body ravaged. Why could he not die? Odin ... please ... forgive him for all ... just spare him this.

Starkad could stand no more.

But no Ás answered his prayer. Starkad, more than any other, knew the truth. The Aesir and Vanir had never been gods. They didn't answer prayers. They didn't even fucking hear them. The only real god he knew of was Hel herself, and she had no mercy.

And without mercy, without the peace of oblivion, all that was left was to keep going. A shallow gasp escaped him as he gained his feet.

He caught himself against a tree trunk. Rested there a moment. And then pushed on.

He didn't know where he was going. Maybe it didn't even matter. He just had to keep moving. Just hope to find something ... somewhere he could finally rest.

A howl ripped through the forest. Another answered, and another.

Wolves. Shit.

He glanced up at the enormous, perilous moon. Oh ... well fuck. Varulfur? Starkad *hated* varulfur.

Grunting, he shambled deeper into the wood.

More howls sang out, a whole chorus of them, closing in around him from all sides.

And him without blades or armor or even a pair of gods-damned pants. Keep moving. Faster—just had to stay ahead of them until he could find a place to hide.

He broke into a shuffling trot, heedless of the pain of tromping barefoot through the wood or the noise he made. No man outran a varulf. Not in the long term. But if he could find shelter ...

The howls sounded again, closer. Followed by growls off in the woods to his left.

Godsdamn it. He turned, heading right, sprinting as best he was able, though each breath felt apt to tear his throat and lungs apart.

Starkad blundered into a clearing and stumbled onto a cluster of people. A naked, dark-haired man, set off against Tyr and ... Mother.

Mauled corpses everywhere. Growls and snaps from the woods. Screams as men and women were torn apart.

The varulf—Fenrir—had Mother by the throat.

"No!" Starkad shrieked. He raced forward to stop it, but his limbs had shrunk. He was a mere boy, a helpless child. "No!"

He raced for her.

As he closed in, Fenrir's hands became claws, his face shifting, becoming lupine. He jerked his hands apart, claws ripping through Mother's throat. They shredded flesh like scythes through grain. Blood exploded out of Mother's throat and drenched Starkad's face.

He stumbled, wailed, and fell to his knees.

No ... No ... No ...

Not again.

Not *again*.

Growls echoed from the woods all around. Trembling, Starkad turned to the shadows. So many sets of yellow eyes, staring hatred at him. Stalking closer.

Tyr was gone.

Fenrir was gone.

But a half dozen of Fenrir's children yet remained. Snarling at him.

The sharp cry of a storm petrel jolted him. He turned, tearing his gaze from the wolves closing in. The bird rested nearby, sitting upon the pommel of a sword stuck in the ground. Its pommel was shaped like a raven's head. Its blade bore runes like Tyrfing or Skofnung.

With a desperate cry of rage, Starkad lunged for the blade. Caught it in one hand.

This wasn't right. He hadn't been so young back then. He'd passed fifteen winters. And hadn't even been there when Mother ...

Starkad jerked the blade from the dirt and spun on the circling wolves. He was no child, but a man. He was not naked, but fully clad and armored in mail. And he was beaten ... but far from broken.

A wolf charged him.

Starkad bellowed and raced to meet it. His blade flashed, tore through the wolf's muzzle and split its skull in a single swipe. Another of the pack leapt at him. Starkad whipped the runeblade around and decapitated the wolf.

More of them closed in. It became hard to keep them all

in view, especially with no peripheral vision in his left eye. That left only overpowering them with sheer fury. He roared at them, blade flashing in the moonlight, every move tearing varulfur to pieces. Again and again he spun, whipping the blade in tight arcs of death. The varulf corpses piled up.

A dozen dead.

Starkad roared challenge at the woods. More and more wolves poured from it, and he raced to meet them all. His blade punched clean through an open maw and tore out the top of a wolf's skull as he jerked it free. Spun it down through the ribs of another and severed its spine. He whipped it around, cut through more and more of the pack. His fury lent him speed and endurance like he'd never known.

And then the pack broke, scampering off into the woods, yelping and fleeing like cravens.

Starkad pointed the blood-drenched runeblade at the moon and bellowed defiance at the varulfur.

Finally, deprived of foes, his strength fled. His arms dropped limp to his sides, and he struggled, panting for breath.

His legs still ached. His flesh was sore and seared. His throat and arse felt scraped raw. He was still blind in one eye.

And as he turned, his mother's mutilated corpse still lay among the dead wolves.

Starkad shut his eyes, trying to block out the sight. When he opened them, the horror yet remained. No reprieve, even if the sword had saved him from being torn apart.

But had the wolves caught him, slain him, would he then have had peace? He stared at the raven-pommel and the bird's lifeless eyes stared back. Was this faint hope but one more torture? Did the Otherworlds taunt him by dangling a thread before him just when he lay on the precipice of utter despair?

Shaking his head, he stalked from the clearing, trying not to look upon Mother's still form.

Maybe he was not broken.

But he could not hide from the truth—one day soon, he would be.

15

Sometimes, in the long stretches as they trekked through the uninhabited wilderness of Kalevala, Hervor imagined what Starkad must see in the nightmares the mara inflicted upon him. Perhaps he saw a sky not unlike the one that now loomed above.

Thunder rumbled within roiling dark clouds that stretched out as far to the north as she could see. They cast Pohjola—for she had no doubt they had reached its threshold—into a shroud of perpetual gloom. A place for nightmares, without doubt. Despite the summer, ahead the land was covered in unmelted snows, trapped in cold and darkness.

As if she stared into the world of Hel herself. And strode boldly within.

A bolt of lightning streaked across the sky, so bright it stung her eyes. Left white flashes on her periphery for a moment.

Hervor tightened her cloak around her shoulders. A fell wind howled down from the north.

Pakkanen pointed at something beyond her sight. "The North Star lies ahead, across many miles of this."

"How can you even tell? It's daylight—to say naught of that thundering mass obscuring the sky."

"I can tell."

Well. That cleared things right up. It was why he was here, she supposed. She sniffed. "Fine. Lead the way. Best not waste a moment."

Gylaug pulled up beside her and addressed Pakkanen. "So word tells it, Kvenlander, the women in this land have beauty what would make the alfar themselves weep for it."

Latham chuckled. "Sounds like something I'd fancy a look at. Maybe a long look at several. Give them a look at my weeping alfar, too."

Hervor rolled her eyes. "Are you sure the only reason you're not a skald is your archery skills? Because your way with words oft leaves me speechless."

Latham pointed at her. "Right you are. Need help with that, we can just step around behind that tree and get it done quick as you like. I can't help but imagine we'd both feel better about life afterward, and that's a fact."

Hervor spit.

Pakkanen stared expressionlessly at Latham until the mercenary found somewhere else to look. "Many have come to these lands seeking brides. Men wiser, stronger, and faster than any of you. Few made it back, and none quite unchanged. Take these kingdoms in jest, and they will make their warnings out of your tale."

Gylaug slapped Latham on the back. "Never know when to stop talking, do you?"

Latham shrugged. "It's a gift."

Hervor trod out onto the snows crunching under her feet. They didn't seem deep here, but from the looks of it, the snows would only increase as they pushed onward. The pain in her ribs and jaw was less these days, though she could have done with a moon or so of rest. Not like to get that any time soon though.

Ecgtheow trotted up beside her while the others trailed behind.

Hervor cast him a bitter glance. Once, she'd actually liked Tiny. Now ... Maybe he'd never understand why she had to do what she did. Once or twice, on the road, she'd tried to explain, but he wasn't hearing it. "What do you want?"

"To remind you why we're here, lest the pirates' misplaced merriment distract you."

She scoffed. "We're here for Starkad. You think *I* am one to be distracted from my purpose?"

"We're here because you murdered a man and he's still enacting a slow, cold revenge. Don't suppose I even want to know what he'll come up with next. Don't much suppose you'll be the only one to suffer for it, either. Kind of makes a man wonder, though, if it would all stop once you died."

Odin's godsdamned balls, was she sick of his judgments. "Go fuck a troll," she snapped, just quiet enough no one behind ought to have caught wind. "You're here for the same reason I am—to help Starkad. And you, my *friend*—you were right there helping Jorund try to take over Sviarland as I recall. You manage that with no blood on your hands?"

Ecgtheow cast a glance back at the others. "True enough. We're all murderers and worse, every one of us. Three pirates I wouldn't otherwise trust to paint a hall. A shaman who's no doubt mist-mad from poking around in the Otherworlds. And Wudga ... Well, we both know who he was serving not so very long ago."

"Then stop judging me and start helping."

Ecgtheow spat out into the mist, then waved a torch to displace it as they pressed on. "Not a one of us can pretend to be clean, I'll grant you. Don't suppose any of us can even claim to be good people. But—far as I know—you're the only here who stabbed a member of her own crew in the back. Takes a special kind of betrayal to motivate a man to rise from the grave to avenge it, I imagine."

Oh, Hel take him. "I did what I had to do to avenge my kin. If you cannot understand that, that's your godsdamned problem."

The man grunted, shook his head and fell back with the others.

Hervor pressed on further ahead, torch out in front of herself. No, her little crew might not have had overmuch love for one another. But Ecgtheow wasn't exactly doing much to make things better, either. He was a strong fighter, an asset in this place—if he could get his priorities straight. If she could somehow make him focus on Starkad and not on her.

She'd done what she had to do. The Arrow's Point had needed to die. Her mistake wasn't murdering him—it was forgetting to torch his corpse. Had she done that, she wouldn't be mired in this troll shit now.

The wind seemed almost to respond to her mood, howling more fiercely. Biting at her cheeks, even through the protection of her furs.

Maybe some of this was her fault. Maybe. Somehow, though, she kept finding herself pushing beyond the bounds of Midgard. And that always seemed to come back to Starkad. So maybe that was part of his curse. He'd warned her she'd get caught up in it.

She didn't know what to think anymore. All she could say for certain was, she was cold as Hel's arse. And she wasn't going to stop, no matter what. A witch needed killing, and she'd see it done.

The clouds broke overhead, flinging fresh flurries of snow. Sharp bits of ice smacked her exposed brow like bee stings. Hail? Troll shit. She threw up her arm to shield her face as best she could.

From behind, Latham shouted, cursing the sky, the gods, and apparently his ex-wife or former lover.

16

The farther they travelled north, the hillier the land became. Ecgtheow supposed they'd be breaking into full-blown mountains before much longer. He couldn't say the thought of climbing mountains in the cold, dark land much appealed, but the land hadn't asked his opinion.

The tree cover was lighter here in Pohjola than down in Kalevala—scattered pines and evergreens and so forth— enough to obscure the view of the sky but not enough to slow their progress overmuch. Between the woods and the dark and the mist, though, he was only half sure they were even still headed the right way. Pakkanen didn't seem to have much doubt, though, just pushing on like he was guided by some fey instinct Ecgtheow didn't care to know much about.

Still, probably for the best they had him. Ecgtheow would not have wanted to find himself wandering around lost in a place like this.

"I swear on my left foot," Latham said, "this land grows

darker with every passing hour. At this rate, I won't be able to see my cock when I piss this evening."

Kustaa grunted.

Ecgtheow waved the torch about in a vain attempt to dispel the mist. Up here, the stuff seemed almost thick enough to choke on. "Might be best you keep a bit more silent. Don't suppose we want anyone knowing we're coming."

Up ahead, Hervor snorted. "Latham won't even keep silent when he's dead."

And she'd know about the dead talking, wouldn't she? Ecgtheow bit back the urge to snap at her. Their little group had enough mistrust between them as it was, without him spitting in the pot.

"All of you, quiet," Gylaug snapped from somewhere off to the side. The pirate didn't have a torch, so Ecgtheow couldn't make him out.

"Now captain," Latham said, "best if you keep the requests reasonable. You know—"

"Quiet! Listen."

Ecgtheow froze in mid-stride, then settled his foot down in the snow, slow as he could. Still crunched underfoot, sounding louder than ever. Always went like that when you tried to go for stealth. He craned his neck to the side, intent. Didn't hear much but the crackle of flame, the breathing of the others—some still hidden by the mist. More snow crunching as someone turned about.

The wind whistling through the trees. He'd almost managed to forget about that by now. Rough sound, easy to set a man on edge, have him jumping at shadows. Places like this, they made everyone ...

Was that a voice?

No. Just some frog croaking, sound carried by the wind.

Hardly aught he needed to worry over. Except ... there it was again. Bunch of frogs croaking. Irregular sounds, almost like they were talking to each other. Come to think on it, what in Hel's frozen underworld were frogs doing up here in the icy wastes of Pohjola?

"What is that?" Hervor asked. "Is there someone there?"

"Everybody form up tight," Gylaug said. "We don't want to get separated in the mist."

Sure as Hel didn't. Ecgtheow worked his way toward the pirate's voice. "Gylaug?"

"Here."

Ecgtheow followed the sound a moment, then headed for a light nearby. Hervor held a torch, standing beside the pirate. Latham and Kustaa were there, each with torches as well. Pakkanen didn't carry one, instead turning about slowly, peering into the darkness.

At this point, Ecgtheow couldn't rightly say if it was day or night. They just walked a good number of hours, then they slept. Then they walked some more.

The croaking on the wind had grown more frequent, if still faint. Almost couldn't catch it.

"Where's Wudga?" Hervor said.

Damn Otherworldly bastard. Ecgtheow swept his torch around again, but caught no sight of the man. Nor was he like to. Wudga hardly ever carried a damn torch. Man was probably sucking down mist, slowly going mad and losing whatever passed for his wretched soul ... while they stood around with their arses in their hands looking for him.

"We need to keep moving." Pakkanen's voice was a bare whisper now.

Gylaug spat, then pulled a torch and lit it off Kustaa's. "Everybody stay tight on me." The pirate resumed his advance, slightly in the lead, waving his torch back and forth.

"Can't say I much like being stalked," Latham said.

Kustaa grunted.

"Right you are. Arse-wrangling butter snorters ought to come out and face us like men."

Ecgtheow faltered a step, trying to figure out what Latham had even said.

"They are not men ..." Pakkanen's voice seemed far away despite him walking not five feet from Ecgtheow.

"Right you are," Latham said. "They're no men. Cravens is what they are. Cowardly little cockless rats afraid to come out and show themselves. Well, I fear naught, you piss-guzzlers! You hear me? Your croaking is naught to me but the buzzing of a fly." Latham hefted his bow in the air. "A fly about to be skewered!"

Something rustled in a tree to Ecgtheow's side.

He spun, hand on the hilt of his sword. Latham may have been a buffoon, but he was right on one count—this had gone on long enough. Ecgtheow pulled the blade and held it out, torch to one side and sword to the other.

He took a step toward where the rustle had come from. The branches shook, but he saw naught else. "Something up in the trees."

All at once, chaos exploded.

Branches all around shook and trembled, croaks filled the air, and shadows scampered everywhere. Blurred forms scrambled up tree trunks and over the snow.

Behind him, one of the men shouted. Ecgtheow couldn't rightly say who, as he bellowed his own war cry and charged the damn tree.

Someone screamed ahead.

Ecgtheow swept the torch up, hit naught, and spun

around as he felt a rush of air pass just behind him. A hint of a shadowy form darted around him then seemed to vanish from sight even as it flew back toward the tree.

"What the fuck?" He swung his sword and it lodged into the tree, sending a jolt up his arm.

The shadow leapt over him.

An arrow thudded into the tree a foot from his head.

"Damn it," Latham said before Ecgtheow could even object to him shooting so close. "They're too fucking quick!"

Ecgtheow spun, yanked at the sword, but it was stuck fast. His torchlight washed over the shadowy creature for a bare instant, enough to catch sight of a hunched-over form, misshapen and twisted. Hardly a clear view though, and then it shimmered like water and was gone again.

A sharp pain lanced through his left leg as claws tore into it. Screaming, he stumbled to one knee, banging that against a root.

He tried to rise, and a form leapt off the tree and collided with him. The impact bore him down onto his back, wedging him into the snows. The torch landed beside him. Whatever it was, it was smaller than him but at least as strong. Ecgtheow wrestled with the creature, tried to throw it off.

Didn't weigh overmuch, but it was fast as a wolf and tough as one in the bargain. They tumbled end over end and the thing came up on top. Vicious claws lanced down and tore through his cheek, scraped over his teeth, and ripped open his gums.

He gurgled, choking on blood as he tried to scream at the pain of it. The thing leaned in, baring pointed teeth nigh as long as his fingers. It had bulging eyes, frog-like, and warty skin, almost yellow. Slick, slimy, except in protruding ridges.

It pushed an oversized hand down on his face, covering his eyes. Its palm was almost big enough to wrap around his whole head, and its clawed fingers dug into the base of his skull. Ecgtheow flailed, tried to throw it off him again.

Fangs sunk into his shoulder, tore through his mail. Burned like acid as the creature gnawed and ripped out flesh.

A war cry above.

Ichor sprayed over him and the slimy creature collapsed atop him, fangs still embedded in his arm. Ecgtheow bellowed in the awful pain of it, but managed to dislodge the beast and throw it off.

Latham was there, a battle-axe lodged in the creature. The pirate jerked the blade free, then offered Ecgtheow a hand. Ecgtheow took it, then winced through a haze of pain as Latham yanked him to his feet.

"No shooting these arse-wranglers ..." He glanced around. "Move!" The pirate shoved him forward. "Run!"

Ecgtheow stumbled, almost fell. Shit. Troll shit! He faltered, then turned back and grasped the hilt of his sword with both hands. Fresh pain shot through his shoulder as he yanked the blade free of the trunk. He slumped against the tree for a heartbeat. Two.

Then transferred his sword to his left hand—right was nigh to useless at the moment. He trotted off in the direction of flickers of torchlight.

Croaking sounding from all around them.

Closing in from all angles of the forest.

Latham grabbed him by the back of his mail and shoved him faster. "Not a place we want to be, my friend!"

Ecgtheow stumbled, barely able to keep his feet. His leg tried to give under him. Blood dribbled down his arm and trickled from his fingers into the snow. It oozed from his rent cheek and soaked the front of his mail. His breath hissed chill out of the hole in his face.

Latham grabbed his left arm to steady him, then guided him on.

Pirate was right. Pain didn't matter. They had to get clear of these *things*.

17

*H*igh above, an owl hooted, flying in front of the oversized moon. Starkad shook his head. The bird had circled for an hour, it seemed to him, as he made his way through the endless woodlands. Whatever it sought, it clearly had not found it.

As he'd walked—long now—he'd heard the growls of more varulfur. They did not approach him. Perhaps they knew what he'd done to the others of their kind with his new runeblade. He could not quite say whether not having to slay more of their kind relieved or disappointed him.

The tree cover grew lighter still, eventually giving way entirely to a sandy beach broken by light overgrowth and tall grasses. And beyond, beneath that giant moon, the sea crashed upon the shore.

Starkad paused, staring out over the ocean. Nowhere left to go, now. He could follow the shoreline, of course, maybe find a human village. A vain hope, though, given it truly seemed he'd wandered into the Otherworlds. He was almost certain he was dead, though he could not fathom how through the haze of his memories.

Walking here, his thoughts had drifted oft to Hervor. It was a blessing she wasn't here, though he missed her. At least that meant she must yet live. That, he could be grateful for, if little else.

In the distance, a rocky precipice rose up by the sea, and beyond that, cliffs. No reason to believe there was aught there, but then, no reason to stay here either.

With a shrug and a sigh, Starkad started for the rocks. As he drew nigh, the barks of seals filled the night air, a chorus of them. Maybe he could catch and cook one ... though for some odd reason he was not much hungry. It felt years since he'd eaten, but his body craved naught. Did the dead not require food?

Perhaps not.

On the nearby shore, a trio of seals flopped out of the sea. One barked at him.

Starkad grimaced. Curse him for a fool. If he was in the world of varulfur ... he was in the World of Moon. The world also of finfolk.

He reached for his sword over his shoulder.

At once, the seals charged forward, hopping at odd gaits. Their forms shifted, tails splitting into awkward legs and fins becoming hand-like. They failed to become quite human in form, though, remaining some vile cross between seal and man.

Starkad jerked the runeblade free, twisted, and cut down the nearest of the seals. More of them were emerging from the sea. He should've known. Should've prepared for this ... somehow his head wasn't working right in this realm.

More of the seals surrounded him. He killed again and again. Already, eight of them lay cleaved into pieces around him.

One of the creatures plowed bodily into him. Its toothy

maw snapped down on his hamstring and he screamed at the pain as it gnawed. Its weight sent him toppling to the sand. He tried to bring up the sword, but another of the creatures jumped atop him. That one's teeth sunk into his side.

Another bit down on his ankle. Starkad roared with the pain of it, but the seals weighed too much. There were too many of them. The one that had him by the ankle dragged him through the sand. He flailed, leaving a canal a foot deep. His fingers dug rivets into the beach, doing naught to forestall the seal's intent.

Starkad kicked it in the face, and its head jerked back. Its mouth didn't open, so its teeth ripped at his tendons.

Hands of extraordinary strength seized him by the shoulders and pushed, driving him closer to the sea. A rushing wave washed up over him, covering him to the waist. Saltwater stung the wounds the seals had given him.

Another jerk on his ankle, and he was pulled all the way under. The sea burned his eye. Water shot up his nose and scorched his sinuses. Hands wrapped around his gut—far stronger than any human—and squeezed. What little air was in his lungs exploded outward, and he sucked down great mouthfuls of water.

They pulled him deeper and deeper. Drowning him like prey.

His body convulsed, rebelling at the waters filling him. He thrashed, desperate to reach the surface. But the finfolk just kept dragging him farther underwater. Hundreds of feet. Beyond any hope of ever seeing life-giving air again.

Surrender.

Finally, maybe he would have respite.

His vision dimmed as death seized him. The convulsions slowed.

Time slowed.

Even the horror of it began to fade.

And then it jolted back into stark relief, as if someone had infused air into him once more. And he was drowning all over again. Bubbles flew from his mouth though he shouldn't have had breath left. Water crushed him anew.

Fresh convulsions. Fresh terror.

Over and over they drowned him. Each time, he swore he'd not fear it. Not again. Swore he wouldn't care.

Lied to himself.

His lungs filled back up so the waters could torment him once more. But the sea swept down, washed away from him, and left him kneeling on rocks. Starkad retched up great heaving gulps of seawater. Retched, until his stomach clenched and locked him in dry heaves. Until he collapsed down on the rock and lay still.

Barely able to moan.

Something shook his shoulder. Starkad groaned, refusing to open his eye, refusing to accept further torment from the Otherworlds. He had had enough. He'd ...

Despite himself, he pushed off his hands and met the gaze of the man accosting him.

Afzal Ibn-Hakim.

Another trick. A foul one. Starkad lunged forward and wrapped his hands around the imposter's neck. His weight bore the other man down and he squeezed, his bellow of rage more of a hissing wheeze. He threw all his fury into it.

A seal barked, flopping toward him.

Starkad released the other man, lunged at a nearby rock, and hefted it up, finally looking about his surroundings. A cave ... an undersea cave with a pocket of trapped air. A seal wiggling over slick rocks, barking at him with obvious anger.

And Afzal, gasping, choking, rubbing his throat. The man waved the seal off and the creature paused. "Naliajuk ..." Afzal rasped.

The seal snapped at Starkad, but did not advance further.

"You are not real," Starkad's own voice sounded as scratchy as Afzal's.

Afzal rose to sit, one hand still on his throat. "I am dreaming ... as are you."

"D-dreaming?" Starkad shook his head. "No. I have been wandering, trapped, for ... years. Everything is so fuzzy. I can't remember details, but ..."

"You cannot remember ..." Afzal coughed. "Because it is a dream ... brother. Time ... has less meaning."

"It's not real?" All of this torment had been a dream? That sounded impossible. Why could he not wake? No ... he was dead. And Afzal was a new deception.

"It's real enough." Afzal coughed again. "Your mind and soul are here. A weaker man would've perished already. Something is dragging you from one spirit world to the next."

Starkad rubbed his face. His head was so damn full of mist. It sounded possible. It also sounded like one more nightmarish torment devised to tempt him with false hope. Like that runeblade he'd had ... some time ago. When was that?

"Listen to me, brother. I don't have much time. You drifted into Naliajuk's world and she helped me reach you here. We followed you to the World of Water that your people called Noatun. But we cannot remain here."

"Noatun?"

"Mer and other powers would come for us here. They'll come for you, as well."

"Can you ..." Starkad swallowed. No more false hope. No more torture. "Can you help me?"

He shook his head. "She doesn't have the power to break the hold on whatever traps you in the Spirit Realm. But we can try to guide you out of this world. Maybe if you can push through the remaining worlds ..."

Spirit worlds. Muspelheim and Niflheim ... Svartalfheim. And Afzal's suggestion was to try to brave them all? "You jest."

"It's all Naliajuk could think of. You must find whatever spirit holds your soul here and confront it."

Starkad groaned. "When you say it is powerful enough to drag me through a nightmare trek along every spirit world? How am I to fight such a formless, hateful foe?"

Afzal glanced at the seal—Naliajuk, apparently. "I cannot fight your battles for you, brother. And you cannot afford to linger in one place. These worlds will close in around you and destroy you. If your soul breaks before you can overcome your captor ..."

Starkad crawled over to where the man sat and nodded grimly. If his soul broke, it would be the end of him. But it had become *if*. Afzal had offered him a faint hope once more, assuming he spoke true, assuming this was not one more trick. He clasped Afzal's forearm. "I have missed you."

"And I, you."

Something bellowed outside the cave, a tremendous roar that bubbled out of the waters and made the cavern tremble.

Afzal jerked his head in that direction, then back to Naliajuk. "Go with her. She'll take you as far as she can. She cannot cross from this world—save back to the World of Moon—but she can take you close to a boundary. Your untethered soul may pass into the next sphere."

"But—"

Another roar.

"Go!"

Dammit. Starkad turned to where Naliajuk had already leapt into the water. He jumped in with her and—admittedly with some trepidation—wrapped his arms around her throat.

A powerful twist of her tail sent them diving into the waters, barely giving Starkad the chance to hold his breath. She sped him past cavernous tunnels he'd not even noticed on the way in, and then out, into open waters.

Little light pierced the depths, but he saw shadows passing around him. Shadows the size of cities. Benthic creatures of unimaginable bulk and power.

Naliajuk hurtled the pair of them through the waters, past those shadows. She banked, turning at a nigh vertical angle, and raced upward.

On and on waters streamed past him. His ears popped. His lungs expanded, feeling apt to burst at any moment. A bright light glared at him from above.

Naliajuk wriggled free of his grasp, spun around and stared at him. His lungs were on fire. The seal jerked her head upward.

Unable to spare her even another heartbeat, Starkad swam straight up.

18

*E*very step was pain. Ecgtheow wanted to collapse and lie in the snow. Of course, he'd bleed to death rather quick that way. Then again, if he kept running, that would still happen.

"What the fuck are they?" Hervor rasped, seeming almost as breathless as he felt.

The creatures kept hitting them then disappearing into the mist. At first, he wasn't sure, thought it was a trick of the darkness or something. But now he'd seen two more of them. They seemed like they could actually turn invisible, or something nigh enough to it. Little shits weren't even five feet tall—not hunched over like that—but how did you fight what you couldn't see?

"Hiidet," Pakkanen answered Hervor, as if that explained aught.

Ecgtheow was hardly in much shape to fight. If not for Latham, he'd be dead already. The pirate had killed another one of these things. Abominations were harrying every step they took though.

Half their crew had wounds from those claws. And here,

Ecgtheow felt flush, feverish, like every step ought to be the last; he pitched forward and splattered his bloody face in the snows.

"K-kill us ... all ..." His words hissed out of the hole in his cheek. Dizzy. Hard to think ...

Gylaug pushed forward, guiding their passage, though Ecgtheow doubted he knew where they were going. Away from the croaks, he supposed. The creatures may have looked like frogs, but they scrambled up trees like fucking lizards.

"What are hiidet?" Gylaug demanded.

"Land vaettir," Pakkanen said. "They come up from the ground."

Popping out of rocks or something? Ugh. Ecgtheow was going to retch. He had to stop. He had to stop.

Except Latham kept on pushing him.

"Tales say they take victims underground. Some they eat ... some they ... make like them. Try to come inside you."

Latham spit. "Can't say I want any frog man thing inside me. I'm too pretty for eyes like that."

"Then move faster," Gylaug snapped back at him.

The pirate did, pulling Ecgtheow along until his legs gave out beneath him. He slumped down, pulling Latham to the ground beside him. "I c-can't ... I can't ..."

"Odin's balls," Hervor said. "Get up, Tiny."

Even Pakkanen was bent over, hands on his knees, panting. How long had they been running? An hour?

Gylaug grumbled, doubling back behind Ecgtheow. He swept his torch around, as if he was going to see an invisible monster out in the mist. "Catch your breath. Just a moment, mind. We cannot allow them to catch us." Pirate was scratching so furiously at his scar it had started bleeding.

"They're herding you." The voice came from the mist.

Wudga stalked forward, sword in hand, that dripping with black blood. "They drive you deeper into the hill country."

"Herding?" Latham said. "I'm not a sheep."

"We can't let that happen," Hervor said. "Wudga, you killed a hiidet? You know something of them."

"A hiisi," Pakkanen wheezed, as if naming the shits mattered in the least at the moment.

"Kobolds," Wudga said. "That's what they call them in your lands."

Kobolds? Fucking children's stories as far as Ecgtheow knew. Except, children's tales don't usually rip out your face nor bite through to your shoulder. "K-kill ... them."

Wudga moved to Ecgtheow's side, then rustled through his own pack before pulling out some cloth and ceramic vial. "They're vaettir. You can only kill their hosts. If they can, they'll drag you down and take your body as a vessel. Whatever they've inflicted on you now will pale before the horror of serving their twisted whims." He uncorked the vial and an acrid smell reached Ecgtheow.

Though he tried to pull away, Wudga grabbed him and poured the vial over his wounded shoulder. It stung for a heartbeat or two. Then it burned like Wudga had dumped acid over him. Ecgtheow shrieked as his flesh sizzled and popped. Wudga slapped a hand over his mouth and shoved him up against a tree, held him there while the burning spread. Ate his flesh, by the feel of it.

Ecgtheow pushed at him, but with one arm, he couldn't match Wudga's strength.

"What in Hel's crotch are you doing?" Latham demanded.

"He's losing too much blood. All of you are. The blood excites them. And their bite carries virulent diseases. If we don't treat this, he'll weaken until he falters. And then he'll be a ripe host for one of them."

Ecgtheow thrashed at that. He sure as the gates of Hel didn't want those things inside him. Not them, not any vaettr.

Finally, the burning eased off. Wudga removed his hand, then began to wrap the cloth around Ecgtheow's shoulder.

"We can't let them herd us," Hervor said again, as if anyone had forgotten. Her scratchy voice grated on Ecgtheow's nerves. She was half bent over, too, holding her ribs again. "We have to push through them and break free in another direction."

"She's right," Wudga said. He tore off another piece of cloth and set to binding Ecgtheow's leg.

Gylaug scoffed. "Easy to say. We cannot fight such monsters. We have barely survived thus far. A head-on assault—"

"Is our only chance," Hervor said, then grunted in obvious pain herself. "You heard Pakkanen and Wudga. These creatures will hunt us down one by one and use our bodies. You think we want to go wherever they're leading us? Into an ambush, perhaps? Maybe there's more of them where we're headed."

Ecgtheow groaned at even the slight relief Wudga's ministrations had given his shoulder and leg. Still felt like his guts were burning him from the inside out—too much to hope that would go away. "Don't suppose … we have overmuch option, really." Loath as he was to agree with Hervor. "Wherever they want us, we … don't much want to be there."

Latham chuckled as if aught about this was the least bit amusing. "Right you are, then. Instead of where they're herding us, we charge them and let the shitters send us to the gates of Hel. I feel fair certain that's a nicer, warmer place than here."

"I've made my decision," Hervor snapped. Had she? And who the fuck put her in charge? "We push through, hard and fast, before they can change tactics."

Gylaug looked about at each of them, nodded, and drew his seax. "Let it be done, then."

19

*T*yrfing gleamed with fell fire, a light obscured by the thick black blood coating its blade. Hervor panted, wobbled in place over the fallen hiisi, and took another faltering step forward.

Ahead of her, more cries of battle. Fleshy *thwacks* as swords and axes bit into hiisi flesh. Screams, as claws rent men to pieces.

These trollfuckers were all but endless.

Torch in one hand, runeblade in the other, Hervor raced forward. Gylaug came into view, a pair of hiidet atop him, slashing and rending while he thrashed in a vain attempt to dislodge them. One had him by the leg and was dragging him away.

Hervor bellowed—or tried, since it was more of throaty growl at this point. The one on the pirate's leg turned its head. Tried to leap away. Almost fast enough.

Tyrfing sheared through its gaping maw and out the back of its skull, lopping the top of its head clean off. She whipped her sword around.

The other hiisi leapt off Gylaug, shimmering and

vanishing in mid-air. A light thump as it hit a tree trunk. Must've been scrambling upward given how the boughs shook. Hervor launched herself at the tree and swung. Her blade sliced cleanly half a foot deep into the trunk but hit no flesh.

A shadow from the corner of her eye. She spun, trying to bring her sword back up. A solid mass slammed into her chest and bowled her over. She landed in the snow, dropped her torch, and struggled to get her arms up to protect her face.

Claws slashed at her almost too fast to see. Rent through the mail on her forearm and tore flesh straight down to the bone. Fuzzed her head with a haze of pain. She was shrieking in horror, in agony.

Black blood splattered her face. She could barely see its source in the chaos. Gylaug's seax was embedded in the hiisi's shoulder. The creature shrieked, spun on the pirate, tearing the seax from his grasp. It leapt at him. One of its claws caught him in the face and he fell, screaming, clutching both hands to the wound.

Gasping, Hervor lunged forward with Tyrfing, drove the blade through the hiisi's back and out its chest. The thing shuddered and railed. Wiggled as it tried to free itself. Should've been dead. Should've been really fucking dead.

Gylaug's seax was still lodged in its shoulder.

Hervor grabbed that with her right hand, the twinge of pain in her shoulder naught compared to the pain in her forearm. She jerked the blade free and cleaved it down into the back of the hiisi's skull before it managed to slide off Tyrfing. The creature finally fell still and slumped down to the ground.

"My eye!" Gylaug was wailing. "My eye!"

Oh Hel.

Tyrfing squelched against the hiisi as Hervor jerked it free, her teeth grit against the pain in her right arm.

Naught much she could do for Gylaug at the moment. Still wobbly, she forced herself to head toward the next flickering torch, the screams of battle.

Kustaa was there, axe swinging round in great mighty strokes that would no doubt leave the man exhausted—assuming he hadn't passed that point some time ago.

Ecgtheow had fallen and Pakkanen was half-dragging the man away while Latham tore into a pair of hiidet with his battle-axe. Utter chaos.

Hervor charged in and swiped with Tyrfing. The runeblade caught a hiisi under the ribs and bit through, deep enough to hit spine. Black blood oozed over her hand as she yanked the blade free. Felt like her arms were turning to water. Like they'd just fall clean off her shoulders.

She turned.

Caught sight of a shimmer flying through the air at Latham's back. She'd opened her mouth, tried to shout a warning that came out as a rasp. The hiisi collided with Latham, sent him stumbling forward into the path of the one he was fighting. That one slashed its claws right over his gut. Latham doubled over, even as the one on his back sank claws into his shoulders.

"No!" Hervor screamed, running for him.

Those oversized teeth sunk down on the back of his neck. The sickening sound of bone crunching hit her as Latham's screams fell silent almost instantly. The hiisi jerked its head from side to side, then back. Ripped a chunk of Latham's spine out. The pirate's head lolled limp to one side, held on by naught but a strip of skin and muscle. The hiisi rode him down as he fell, still ripping into him with claws.

Hervor's stomach lurched. She stumbled and had to steady herself. Then back up, charging. Tyrfing gleaming as it cleaved into Latham's murderer. The runeblade sheared through its arm and into its neck.

The disfigured monster pitched over, clawed hands now wrapped around its own throat.

The other one leapt at her before she could get the blade back up.

She saw it, seeming to fly through the air. A distorted shimmer of claws and fangs and slimy yellow flesh. Her death in its bulging eyes.

Wudga came out of nowhere. His runeblade caught the monster in mid-air and sliced it almost straight down the middle. The two halves landed to either side of Hervor, showering her in gore and blood. Bits of intestine hit her in the face. Slimy fluid stung her eyes.

Unable to stop herself, she bent over and retched up what little remained in her stomach. Her gut kept clenching.

Alive ... she was alive.

She was alive.

Her hair was plastered to her face with blood and she didn't want to know what else. Obscuring her vision. Looking up through it, Kustaa was cutting down a hiisi. As another closed in on him.

Odin's giant balls! "We ... we cannot push through," she rasped. "Retreat."

No one really looked to her, save Wudga. Probably couldn't even hear her words over the chaos and slaughter. The men dying on her mission.

"Retreat!" Ecgtheow bellowed, his voice wheezing through the hole in his face. "Retreat!"

At least someone heard her. He caught her eye, glared at

her. At least for the instant before Pakkanen pulled him away. The man blamed her for all this. For Latham's death.

And he should.

Fuck!

Gasping at the pain, she stumbled after Ecgtheow and Pakkanen. A glance back at Kustaa ... He and Wudga were making a fighting retreat, following them.

Gylaug was up when she reached him, struggling to move forward with one hand still clasped over his right eye.

"Move!" she shouted, caught his arm, and dragged him onward.

Straight into whatever madness the hiidet had wanted them in the first place.

THE DARKNESS ONLY DRAGGED ON. It had to be night—almost pitch black save for the torches, and those barely cut through the mist here. The hiidet continued to harry them every step. Except, now that they were moving in the other direction, the monsters didn't stick, didn't hold any line.

It removed any doubt Hervor had left about Wudga's observation.

As they pushed into a dale, she came to a tree that was bent and twisted back on itself. Its bark had turned black, looked almost like ash. Rotten to the core.

Hervor gave it a wide berth then almost stumbled into another just the same. So warped its branches scraped the ground and tangled in their own roots. The inside seemed to weep black sap that looked more like tar than aught else.

"We've reached the lands of Hel," Gylaug mumbled.

Hervor turned to him. He had removed his hand from his face. Exposed the gaping hole where a hiisi had torn his eye out. Four red lines marred his face above and below that weeping red void, gouges deep enough some of them probably hit his skull.

If she hadn't already retched, she would have, to look at him. Instead, she forced herself to look ahead. More of the rotten, twisted trees. In fact, it seemed like this whole dale had fallen to some horrific pestilence.

"We cannot travel in such a place," Pakkanen warned. "We court death."

Dozens of croaks sounded out behind them, growing closer.

Dammit! Gods above, she wished Starkad was here. He might know what to do. Hervor swallowed. "We have no choice. They'll tear us to pieces unless we find a place to hide. Wudga!" The man was by her side almost immediately. "Can you find a way through here, a secret route?"

"I'm not sure. This is their place ..."

"Try, damn it." There was no going back the way they'd come, that much was certain. It was forward or death.

Wudga nodded, face grim, and slipped off into the mist.

More croaking, and closer than ever.

Great steaming piles of troll shit. "Move!" Hervor said. "Forward."

The warped trees made navigating the dale like wandering a maze. She had to turn, double back, duck under a tangle. A thorn tore through her trouser and cut into her thigh. Naught compared to the pain and blood loss in her arm though.

She ducked under another overhanging branch that had grown down into the ground. Just keep pushing forward. Just keep moving.

Someone moved past her, through the mist. Kustaa. Didn't even meet her gaze. Did he blame her for Latham?

Hel.

"Over here," Wudga's voice called out from the mist ahead.

She edged forward a bit. The roots and branches were so thick she could barely see a damn thing. "Where?"

"Here. This way."

She followed the voice, ducked under another overhang, and came into a clearing—if you could call a hollow no more than eight feet across a clearing. A slight rock pile had prevented the roots from rising up here, and Wudga sat upon that.

Pakkanen followed, still helping Ecgtheow, but paused when he saw her, gaze lingering on her arm. The shaman shook his head. "I must stitch that before you bleed to death."

Dizziness was already making her wobble. No point in arguing. She stumbled over to the rocks and half-sat, half-collapsed there. Tyrfing clattered against them as it fell from her grasp. The moment she released it, the dizziness increased.

"We have no time for stitches," Wudga said. He pulled a knife and held it in a torch.

Oh ... Odin's lumpy trollfucking balls!

She didn't bother protesting. Wudga was right.

"If the tales are true ..." Pakkanen said. "The hiidet may be in service to a greater power. They seem to be moving with purpose."

Hervor grimaced. "I don't give a flying fuck what their purpose is or whom they serve. Naught will stop me from killing this Loviatar if that's what it takes to save Starkad. I will cut down every last hiisi in Pohjola if needs be." She looked to Wudga. "Do it."

❦

HERVOR HADN'T QUITE BEEN able to stifle her scream as Wudga seared her wound closed. Not that she really thought they'd have been able to rest long in that clearing in any event. The hiidet wanted them moving, clearly.

They pressed on, until the mist itself seemed green tinged and foul-smelling, like it had mixed with sulfur and marsh gas. The ground underfoot began to squelch, no longer snow, but slush and mud and muck.

The further into the dale they pressed, the more bog-like it became.

Beside her, Gylaug suddenly yelped. The pirate disappeared beneath waters deeper than any of them had expected. Only to surface a heartbeat later, thrashing.

Hel.

Gylaug flailed, hands slapping at the uneven surface beside Hervor. She dropped to one knee and reached for his arm. His slick wet hand slipped from her grasp. He slapped again, and she caught him.

Grunted in pain as his weight pulled on her bad shoulder—her bad arm. She caught his wrist with her other hand, then pulled. No purchase, no way to get the pirate back on the semi-solid mud. In fact, he was pulling her in with him. Her feet and knees squelched, slid, closer and closer to the spot he'd fallen in.

Kustaa dropped down beside her, caught Gylaug's elbow, and heaved. With the other pirate's help, they pulled Gylaug up onto the mud, spraying the pair of them with freezing bog water in the process.

Hervor fell onto her back and lay there, panting, heedless of the mud seeping in through her mail. Gods above and below, what she would give for a good night's sleep. Or three.

Voices carried on the wind, like whispers. Not quite the croaking she'd come to expect from hiidet.

Hervor pushed herself up. "What is that?"

Pakkanen turned about slowly. "Many men have died here."

"Ghosts?" she mumbled. Not ghosts.

"Perhaps. There is a presence that hardly welcomes the living."

Didn't need a shaman to know that much. "Up," she said, groaning as she rose herself. "Everyone up. Move. Move now."

Someone—Ecgtheow maybe—out in the mist grumbled under his breath.

And they were pressing on again. What choice remained but forward?

Every step ushered in new aches, twinges of pain, regrets. Maybe ... maybe she'd been a fool to betray Orvar? No. No—he had deserved it ten times over. The murderer had earned the urd that befell him and more. She could not allow agony and anguish to make her doubt herself. Starkad needed her strong. She'd kill Loviatar. And then she'd fucking kill Orvar-Oddr *again*.

Onward they pushed, until they came to a rocky hill rising up like a turtle shell out of the bog. The tree cover was lighter there, roots barely able to break through the stones.

Behind, she heard Gylaug's teeth chattering, clanking together at irregular intervals that grated on her frayed nerves. She ought to have had sympathy, of course. The pirate had lost his godsdamned *eye* for this.

But all she could think of was getting out of this cursed muck and getting dry. Would do him good, too. Panting, she climbed out onto the lowest of the rocks, scrambled to the next, and then the next. Always climbing. Every single fucking time she went somewhere, she was climbing mountains or hills or walls.

Her muck-drenched boots slipped on a rock, skidded, and sent her stumbling to one knee. That banged hard against the stones, sent a jolt of lightning straight from her leg to her brain. Left her groaning.

Kustaa caught her under the arm, heaved her up, and pushed her onward. No rest for any of them.

So she kept on climbing, always upward. She crested the peak of the hill. Only, the top of it dropped inward like a bowl littered with jagged rocks jutting up at every possible angle. Among them, a dozen or so tunnels bored into the hill as if some worm had eaten its way through a giant apple.

What was this? A caldera? The middle of a bog hardly seemed the place for one.

Pakkanen huffed up beside her, stared down, and shook his tattooed face. "Ill omen here."

Yeah, well, all of Pohjola seemed an ill omen as far as Hervor was concerned. Soon as they were done here, Hel could have the whole land back and no one would miss it.

"Are those lava tubes?" she asked. They looked a bit different than the ones she'd seen in Glaesisvellir, but she was no expert on such things.

Pakkanen just frowned, staring at them or something she couldn't see.

She glanced back over the ridge. Gylaug was struggling to climb and Kustaa had gone back to help him. Ecgtheow fared little better, though he'd made it a bit higher. Wudga was missing again, of course.

And from the bog, more croaking.

"The kobolds draw nigh," Ecgtheow said from below, pointlessly.

Hervor looked back to the tunnels. Many were steep, almost vertical, but some bored at an angle they might manage. "We can take shelter in those."

Pakkanen mumbled under his breath before answering. "The hiidet are land spirits. They may well have carved out those passages themselves. Besides, if the tunnels bore down under the bog, they may be flooded in places. Walk there and we may find ourselves trapped."

They were already trapped, in case he hadn't noticed. "Do you have a better idea?"

"Death comes for us now," Gylaug said, teeth chattering even as Kustaa helped him up the rise. "I see ... valkyries ... but choose glory."

Shit. The pirate was losing it. Delirious with blood loss or cold or whatever fever had taken Ecgtheow. For that matter, she wasn't feeling well herself. Still, they needed to—

The rocks in the bowl trembled, and she glanced at them. An instant later, one of the tunnels exploded.

A grayish serpent erupted from the tunnel, gaping maw bigger around than she was. Its reptilian eyes seemed to take in all of them at a single, soul-piercing glance. Had to be a hundred feet long, most of it still buried in the tunnels. A pair of thin forelegs crushed boulders beneath them.

Hervor froze, unable to move. To even think clear. She needed to do something. To scream maybe. That seemed hard right now.

The creature might have looked like a giant snake, except for those two limbs and spiny ridges running along its back. It had strange, wing-like flaps at the back of its head. From behind those hissed a green and black miasma that made her feel ill just to look upon.

"Linnorm!" Gylaug bellowed, jerking his seax free of its sheath.

At his roar, the dragon surged forward, crushing and overturning stones with its momentum. It darted at Gylaug before Hervor could even manage a scream. The dragon's maw snapped shut around the pirate, crunching him and a chunk of the rock he stood on in one fell bite.

Blood gushed out of the dragon's mouth. One of Gylaug's legs flew free. Spinning through the air before splattering on the rocks.

The dragon reared back, swallowed whatever was left of the pirate whole.

Its movement shook the stones and sent Hervor tumbling over backward. The whole world spun, end over end. Rocks banged her shoulder, her legs. Her head. Sent white light blinding her.

A deafening roar.

She was falling. Tried to grab something. Her hand snared on a rock and twisted the wrong way. Back slammed against something sharp. Still tumbling over backward.

She splashed down into the bog and went underwater. Foul muck shot up her nose, scorched her sinuses. She flailed, caught the edge of a rock. Pulled herself upward, burst into air and heaved bog water from her lungs.

Couldn't breathe.

Hurt.

Her torch was gone and she couldn't see a fucking thing through the mist. Water was freezing. Her hands already shaking.

Screams coming from above. Crashes. A rock bigger than she was slammed down not a foot from her face, splintered, and plummeted into the bog. Still screaming ... Oh. That was her.

A thud and a groan sounded a few feet away though she couldn't see what had fallen. Who had fallen, more like. Groaning in pain, she climbed up onto the rocks.

Her heart was stuck in her throat. Dragon ... Not possible.

Dragon ... Linnorm. Stories ...

Tyrfing sat on the rock above where she now knelt, wedged between it and the hill. Water was streaming over her face. Couldn't be sure, but she thought maybe she was weeping with the fear. Absolute terror.

She lunged upward, caught Tyrfing's hilt, and raised it. The moment she claimed it the runeblade flared to light, its pale gleam reflecting off the mist and doing little to improve her vision.

She needed a damn torch.

Where were the others? Dead? All of them?

"Where are you?" Her words were slurred, broken by her chattering teeth. They were all going to die. Devoured by this monstrosity far beyond the lands of men. Mist-madness had brought them here. Her madness. "Where are you, you bastard?"

She sounded like a little girl, crying.

She turned about, slow, runeblade out before her. Maybe she'd die. Maybe. But Tyrfing might be able to slay even a linnorm. She just needed one strong blow.

Something massive splashed down into the bog, sent a wave of icy water sloshing up on to her. Linnorm was in the bog. Swimming, hunting her.

Hervor sucked a shuddering breath in through her nose. She had to run, but where? The mist had blanketed every-thing. She couldn't even make out her feet.

Oh, Odin. Odin, please. Please ...

A hand slapped down over her mouth. She flailed, tried to scream, but arms jerked her to stillness. Then her captor spun her around to face him.

Wudga.

He was alive at least.

Slowly, he withdrew his hand from her mouth, grabbed her wrist, and pulled her after him. The man jumped down from the rock, landing in the mud with a faint squelch. Hervor wished she could have managed half so quiet. Muck splashed around her as she landed.

Wudga jerked her forward, seeming able to navigate the semi-solid ground around them despite the mist.

She wanted to ask about the others but dared not speak, instead letting Wudga silently guide her away from the hill. He paused, crouched low, and she mimicked him.

Ahead of her, unseen, another splash sounded, followed by a rush of water over her shins. Dragon must've swum right past them. Could Wudga see it? Could the dragon see *them*? No ... No, it would have struck already.

Wudga pulled her forward once again, stepped out of the muck and toward a twisted tree. The trunk had split here, spilling the noxious black sap, though most of it seemed to have hardened into an obsidian-like amber. The tree must have once towered high, for the hollow left when it split was a good three feet around. Wudga pulled her inside the opening, up close against himself, and put a hand to her mouth.

Hardly needful. Hervor could not have formed a sentence if her life depended on it.

Outside, the dragon roared again.

Hervor could not stop shaking.

20

*H*is breath was gone.

Water filled his lungs once more.

Desperate, Starkad swam upward through a flurry of bubbles. And then he burst through a veil of water and out into open sky. He spewed water and sucked down precious, beautiful breaths of air.

Treading water, he blinked beneath the blazing sun. It seemed too close now, so bright it nigh blinded his remaining eye. He had to look away, force his gaze lower, and not on the waters reflecting that absolute brilliance. He found himself in the middle of a small lake.

Around it lay a sandy beach dotted by palm trees like those he'd seen on Vanaheim in another lifetime. Other trees spread out beyond them, almost seeming to glitter, like some imagined, pristine paradise. Starkad swam for shore, fighting through the pain in his wounded leg and side.

Before he'd even reached it, a sweat ran along his forehead. This world was blisteringly hot. Not the searing blaze of Muspelheim, perhaps, but a relentless, pounding heat. He pulled himself onto sand that itself burned his hands.

Damn.

Now what? Grunting, he yanked off his mail, then the leather pads beneath it. Damn armor was like to fry him here. In Vanaheim—Asgard—without the mists, the sun sometimes shone so bright it could actually burn your skin if you stayed overlong in it. This world seemed like to achieve that in half the time.

He looked up into the tree line. A whole flock of rainbow-colored birds watched him. Creatures of red and blue and green, more vibrant than aught he'd ever imagined. One in particular—a red and blue-feathered beauty—stared hard at him, spread its wings, and cawed.

Starkad shook his head, still trying to catch his breath. Despite the heat, this world didn't seem so bad thus far. Better, for certain, than aught he'd seen of late. He tried to run back in his mind what worlds he'd passed through, but the memories drifted away like smoke and he couldn't hold on to them.

He'd come from beneath the ocean, he knew that much. That meant ... Noatun, the World of Water. And here, the blinding sun ... Alfheim, perhaps?

Rising, he loosened the laces of his tunic, then trudged off beyond the trees. His leg threatened to give from under him with each passing step.

He wandered through the glittering woods, passing chittering animals that jumped from branch to branch and stared at him. More brilliantly colored birds, as well, all looking down on his passage.

Crashing water sounded in the distance, and he followed its noise. He came to a stream that ran through mild rapids and dropped down over a series of waterfalls. Upstream or down? Starkad scratched his beard, then threw up his hands and wandered up the stream.

This he followed for half of an hour, perhaps, before the trees broke away into a clearing. Within it, fluted marble columns rose up and scraped the sky. Those had to be fifty feet tall, maybe more. They ringed a path that led to an equally massive temple, as if the place had been built for those larger even than jotunnar.

An unpleasant thought, actually.

But still, Afzal had told him he needed to do something. He needed to ... The thought seemed so close he could almost touch it, but it wouldn't stay in his head.

Shit, but he missed his swords. Wandering into such a place unarmed did not much appeal, and less so given he couldn't recall what his intent here was meant to be. Whatever it was, though, it surely lay within.

As he drew closer, he realized the temple had eaves that overhung its walls, but no actual roof. The merciless sun beat straight down through a large atrium, glittering on a pool within. A pool the size of a godsdamned lake. Lush greenery spread out around the pool, even crawling up the interior walls of the temple.

He could not long look at it, though, for the figures in and around the pool demanded his undivided attention. They looked like men and women, true, most naked, the others close to it. Their skins shone so bright they almost seemed to radiate a hint of light, an encompassing aura all around them. Their eyes held the faint glow of sunlight. Some of them bore golden crowns or arm rings that reflected the sunlight, glittering with almost painful brightness.

Never in all his wanderings had Starkad gazed upon such perfection of the human form. Enraptured, he drew closer to the pool, hands limp at his sides. Barely aware he was doing it, he pulled off his shirt and cast it aside.

Then he waded into the waist-deep waters.

The liosalfar drifted closer to him as he approached, forming a ring of beauty around him.

A pair of women drifted forward, and he could not tear his gaze from their perfect breasts. From the pink nipples that begged his worship. From the need to bury his face in one of those bosoms and at last be freed of all his suffering and cares.

He moved toward one of the women, hand outstretched.

Her smile turned to a sneer. "Murderer."

"What?" He faltered.

"Betrayer," she said, now advancing herself.

Starkad backed away, but hands held him in place.

"Touched by the dark," someone behind him said.

"Changed by it."

"Foulness."

"It must be burned pure."

"The sin of shadows runs deep."

Hands lifted him up from the waters, carried him on his back, and he found he had neither the strength nor the desire to resist. They judged him, and he deserved it.

The cloud beneath him became a mighty disc of gold, like a coin the size of a man. His arms and legs were bound to it by glittering golden chains, though he did not remember any of the alfar binding him or even having aught on them with which to do so.

The disc floated several feet above the surface of the water, held him in the dead center of the atrium. The alfar ringed him and sang, their lilting strange voices almost enough to distract him from the sun beating down on him. Its rays heated the gold beneath him until he felt his back sizzling. The skin on his face and exposed arms and stomach began to crisp and blister.

And still the alfar sang.

That blinding light seared Starkad's eye, and yet, while they sang, he could not close it. Could not do aught save stare at the sun, even knowing it would soon burn out his other eye and leave him utterly blind. But that sun demanded his unwavering obedience.

The sun's rays scorched his brain. Seared it as if in punishment for his many crimes. Fiery justice, well-deserved, pouring down on him from the heavens.

A glimmering figure drifted along his periphery, a tall female, lithe as the others. Radiant and glorious. She mounted the disc beside him, then stepped before him, her form blocking out the sun's justice.

Blinking through what little remained of his damaged vision, Starkad stared at her. The perfect, sensuous curve of her jaw. The enrapturing gleam of sunlight sparkling in the irises of her eyes. The sun caught and glittered off her golden hair.

"Ogn ..."

She wore a white dress so sheer it concealed naught at all, with numerous slits allowing it to billow around her in the breeze. Her half smile was enough to restore his faith in life. His love lowered herself, slow and gentle, until her soft hands pressed against his blistering chest. Until her hips rested upon his.

"I've wait so long ..." he mumbled. "So long to see you again. To tell you all things I failed to say ... I just ..."

She smiled, brushing a finger over his lips. Her hands traced along the line of his jaw. Settled beneath it. Closed around his throat. Still smiling, she squeezed. "You denied me this."

Starkad thrashed under her grip, but she had the

strength of the Otherworlds. No mortal could match her glorious power.

"This world, my very birthright among the liosalfar. You denied it to me. Denied me the light." She was still smiling, speaking softly, as if to a lover. But the sunlight had faded from her eyes, replaced by a darkness that seemed to swirl within them. Her sky-blue irises became the color of midnight.

"Driven to madness and utter despair I took my own life and fell, into shadow." She leaned so close, her lips just brushed his own. "Like you. Caught in the dark. Oh, how I waited for you, hungering on the edges of the Veil while my prey lay ever just out of reach."

His vision dimmed from lack of air. It felt like his eye was going to pop from its socket.

Ogn giggled, murmuring. "Can you even imagine my elation when the draug and his pet sorcerer called me forth and set me to my task? I needed but a piece of you ... to drag the pitiful hollow you call a soul into my realm. A hair, taken in simple, meaningless scuffle ... And you were mine. Always and forever."

He strained against the golden chains, tried to reach her. The links refused to give way.

"The longer you hold out, the more entertaining this proves. Please ..." She released him of a sudden and he gasped in air, choked, coughed, and sucked in some more. "Please, dear Starkad. Endure ... Hold on to what is left of your mind. I would long savor the ravaging of it. Given the choice, I would draw out its decay until the end of time."

"What ... are ... you?" he rasped.

She laughed, the sound no longer high and clear as it had been in life, but thick, as if bubbling up through tar. As her laughter rose, the blinding light around him dimmed and gave way to lengthening shadows. The other liosalfar faded away, vanishing like their realm of eternal light.

"Oh," she purred. "Well, I am not a liosalf, thanks to you. Shall I show you the truth of what you wrought from me, my darling? Watch closely then. I'll carry you from horror to horror until naught remains of your wretched soul." She leaned in close. Her teeth had become a maw full of irregular fangs, her tongue an elongated and bulbous thing. She licked it across his face, rough and scraping.

A hideous thought hit him, a memory, that he had lain with this creature before. Many times, that she had sucked his life out of him one lurid encounter after another. As she would now.

She pressed her face against his ear, even as her hands unfastened his trousers, his body responding despite his objections. "By the end, my darling, you may have guessed in what state you have left me. And perhaps …" Her hand closed tight around his cock and stroked it. "Perhaps there will be just enough of you left, to become like me."

21

*H*ow much time had passed? It felt long, quarter of an hour. Maybe twice that. Battle made it hard to keep track of things. Hard to keep your senses. Hervor knew that. Knowing it didn't make it any less confusing.

Wudga had wrapped his arms around her. Probably trying to still her shivering. Maybe just trying to keep her chattering teeth from giving them away.

Everything hurt. The battering on the hillside had bruised her still healing ribs. Even breathing was agony. Blood was seeping through the bandage on her arm, oozing from the wound Wudga had seared closed. Maybe she was lucky to be alive. Didn't feel overmuch like it though.

A shadow hopped and lurched past their hiding place. A hiisi, not quite invisible, as it stalked the bog. Searching for *them*.

Odin's balls. The hiisi served the dragon. She had not seen *that* coming. That creature was the very incarnation of destruction. It was chaos made flesh. She could not imagine aught working *for* it.

"We have to move now," Wudga whispered in her ear. "If we linger too long, they might double back and find our trail."

"F-fire ..." The mist would get inside them, if the cold didn't kill her first.

"We can't. Not here, not yet."

She nodded, lacking the strength to argue. Besides which, Wudga was no doubt correct. If the hiisi spotted her, she'd probably envy Gylaug his swift death. Poor bastard probably hadn't even had time to be scared.

The memory of his leg torn free, flying through the air as the dragon's teeth crunched him ... that thought turned her stomach. Poor bastard.

Wudga led her away from the hill, maybe deeper in the dale, maybe out of it. She couldn't begin to guess their whereabouts anymore. For all Hervor knew, they were headed back out of Pohjola. They *should* be headed out. Coming here had been mist-madness.

But now ... Now Starkad had no other hope left.

Careful of every footfall lest she make a noise, Hervor followed behind Wudga. Every breath she took let the mist inside her. How long did it take to go mist-mad? To lose your soul? Was she there already?

She tried to slow her breathing, but her pounding heart wouldn't cooperate. She was going to die here. Every instinct screamed that inside her head. After everything she'd been through ... she was going to die out here, alone in some bog far from Sviarland.

But the ground beneath them grew drier as Wudga led on, muck giving way to snow once more. Back into the tangled maze of roots and branches and thorns, but Wudga seemed to know where he was going. Of course, when she led men, she pretended to know what she was about even when she didn't have the first clue. Acting confused was a good way to lead to mutiny or panic among a crew.

Maybe Wudga just figured any direction was better than staying nigh to the linnorm. Hard to argue with that, either.

And then, without real warning, a flicker of light shone up ahead. Hervor's steps quickened and rushed past Wudga, barely able to think of aught save fire. Naught else mattered so much as that.

Fire is life.

The others had a small campfire going. Pakkanen, Ecgtheow, and Kustaa. All that were left now, and praise Odin even they lived. Ecgtheow lay on his side, his skin distinctly yellow and putrid looking.

Kustaa was cradling one of his arms. Bruised, maybe even broken. The pirate coughed, shuddered, coughed again and spat out a glob of black phlegm.

"What happened to him?" Hervor asked, knowing how slurred her own words would be.

Pakkanen sniffed, shook his head. "He drew too close to Ajatar."

Hervor collapsed in front of the fire. "Ajatar? The linnorm?"

"I know it by reputation only ... one of the fiends that lurks in Pohjola. A dragon of plague and devastation. An abomination of utmost chaos."

Even after all she'd seen, Hervor had never thought to witness aught like that linnorm. Maybe had never really believed such things real.

Wudga knelt beside her. "Day will break soon. We must use that time."

She snorted. "There's no day here."

"There is, and even if it is not light, it is *lighter*. The hiidet will become less aggressive in the day and this may grant us the only chance to escape this wood. We have but to pray they do not discover this flame before then. Kindling such a thing poses a dire risk."

Ecgtheow murmured something, pushed himself up on his hands and knees, and shook. "Fire ... without fire ..."

"Without fire we'll all be dead anyway," Hervor finished for him.

Pakkanen rubbed his hands together before the flame. "I wish I could say this will be the last horror before us, but I fear otherwise. Perhaps we should retreat while we are still able to do so. The further we press on, the more the Other-worlds are like to bleed into this one."

"No!" Hervor snapped. "I'm not going back without killing Loviatar. We do that, and Latham and Gylaug died for naught."

"They died ... for you ... Press on ... and we may all die for naught," Ecgtheow said.

Hervor flinched. With any luck, the others wouldn't question what he meant when he claimed they died for her. Maybe think he referred to this being her quest. "We all understood what we risked in coming here." Except, she hadn't even begun to guess the horrors they'd faced here. "We—and the fallen—all knew the risks. Naught has changed. We press on, after the North Star, and we finish this."

"Mist-madness," Kustaa said, and spat in the fire.

Everyone stared at him. *Now* he bothered to speak? Hervor rolled her eyes. "Ecgtheow, we faced worse than this on Thule." Probably a lie.

The big man opened his mouth, sputtered, coughed, and gave over whatever argument he'd intended. He was cradling his wounded shoulder. Poor bastard looked like he'd be lucky to live out the day. Then again ... maybe none of them would.

Hervor felt chilled and flushed all at once, shivering and sweating. Light-headed and too nauseated to even consider food. Truth be told, they were all headed down to meet Hel. But if that's what it took ... as long as she killed Loviatar first, Väinämöinen claimed he'd know, and would start the ritual to save Starkad.

She rubbed her face. "When daylight comes, we have to move on, head north. Pakkanen will still guide us. Keep it quiet, keep torches to a minimum. If we can bypass the hiidet without drawing their eyes, we might make it."

Ecgtheow coughed, wheezed. "If ... even one ... spot ..."

She looked to Wudga. "You are adept at sticking to the shadows." And they all knew why. "You must help us skirt around the hiidet."

Wudga stared hard at her. Finally, he nodded.

22

*W*udga was out in front, not far, but farther than Ecgtheow could see through the mist. Pakkanen was just behind, a shadowy silhouette. Ecgtheow supposed the pair of them knew what they were about. Knew which way to go. All a warrior like Ecgtheow could do now was keep his gaze locked on Pakkanen and keep walking.

An hour of sleep had been enough to remind him he was still alive. Mainly because on waking, all the aches hurt fresh. Pakkanen had stitched up his face before he slept. Then given him some draught that tasted like troll piss. Supposed to help with the fevers. Ecgtheow didn't suppose fever was his worst issue though.

He needed a draught that protected him from fucking kobolds and linnorms, was what he needed. That and about three score hours of sleep, a barrel full of mead, and a hunk of well-cooked meat. Mammoth was the best there, sure, but he'd have settled for venison. Pork. Rabbit. Bear. He'd have settled for a damn squirrel if it would've stilled the rumbling in his gut.

Not that he expected he'd be able to keep any of it down if he had it.

Behind him, Hervor and Kustaa brought up the rear. Silent as death, the pair of them. Except for Hervor's occasional stifled coughs. From the look of it, bitch had whatever malady had befallen him. Another day, maybe, and she'd be where he stood now. Small comfort that offered.

Best he could do now was focus on keeping quiet. Last thing they needed was more of those kobold bastards running amok, invisible and vicious as a badger with a thorn in its arse. He'd heard tale of the things, of course. Mostly horror stories out of Nidavellir, men claiming they haunted the mines. Hadn't paid much heed to it though. Who would? Sounded like sailors' fancies about mermaids and sea monsters.

Hel, maybe those were out here too.

A loud croak echoed from off to his right. Another followed behind them. Another to the side once.

"We've been spotted," Hervor said.

Next he knew, that runeblade was gleaming in her hand, flame seeming pale next to the crackling fire of her torch.

Groaning, he yanked his own blade over his shoulder. So much for stealth.

Scampering, just to his side. Couldn't see a damn thing, but the snow crunched, branches rustled. And the croaking.

Hold. Had to wait for them to show themselves. Had to wait …

His lungs felt like they were filled up with rocks. Every breath rattling in his chest like it would crush his heart.

Hold …

A faint shimmer darted just in front of him. A clawed track in the snow. Roaring, Ecgtheow swung at the open air. His broadsword *thwacked* into something invisible and sent black blood splattering his face. The kobold crashed into the snow, its shimmer faded, revealing its wicked bulging eyes.

Thing was already scrambling back to its feet, hissing spittle at him.

Ecgtheow twisted and caught it across the face with his backswing. Tore through a gooey eye and hit the skull beneath. The momentum sent him stumbling forward, crashing atop the creature.

Slime and brains washed over him. He tried to push himself up. His palm caught in goo and he slipped, slapped his face against the abomination. Creature was dead, thank Odin, probably on its way to Hel already.

Ecgtheow rolled over, pushed himself up from the snow and struggled to his feet. More rustling from the trees, shimmering. An almost deafening chorus of croaks. Fucking army of the things.

Behind, Hervor was tearing through them with her runeblade. Sure made him miss Naegling.

Ecgtheow spat. "Come on then."

A shimmer just beside him caught his eye and he spun, swinging. Too high. The creature ducked, plowed into his gut and ripped claws over the back of his hand. His broadsword tumbled from his limp fingers but he managed to heave the creature into the air even as he fell.

The kobold—visible now—spun in mid-air and landed on its feet like a godsdamned cat. Ecgtheow struggled to regain his own, knowing it was too late. He was a dead man. They were all fucking dead.

A bellow erupted from the woods, so loud even the kobold faltered, turning its disgusting face to the noise. A heartbeat later, branches crashed aside as a man—a giant of a man, even to Ecgtheow's eyes—came blundering out. The man slammed right into the kobold, one hand around its slimy throat. His momentum didn't slow in the least as he caught the monster and carried it along.

He just kept charging right up to a tree and rammed the creature bodily into the trunk. And he was still roaring. Before Ecgtheow could do more than drop his jaw, the giant's other hand came up swinging an oversized battle-axe in a wide arc. The blade split the kobold's skull down the middle and wedged into the tree.

Almost at once, the giant man grasped the handle with both hands, yanked it free and spun, clearly intent on finding more foes.

"Höfund?" Hervor rasped from behind Ecgtheow.

He knew his jaw was still hanging limp, but he couldn't think of a damn thing to say. Where in Hel's frozen underworld had this man come from? And how could Hervor possibly know him?

Gaping, he looked back and forth between the two of them.

"Run!" this Höfund bellowed, accent strange and thick.

Couldn't say he needed a second invitation for that though. Ecgtheow snatched up his sword and raced forward, trudging over to where he'd last seen Pakkanen. Seemed a fair time to be anywhere but here.

Blundering through the mist, he almost collided with Wudga. The man's own sword was slick with blood once more. Volund's son was terrifying in the night, it had to be said. What kind of man dealt so handily with the Otherworldly? One with a half a foot in those worlds, Ecgtheow supposed.

Wudga waved him on, pointing to a faint flicker of torchlight. Pakkanen, most like. Ecgtheow kept running, chest heaving, heart feeling apt to burst any moment. Hervor's unexpected friend may have saved them for now, but Ecgtheow still didn't expect to see nightfall. His whole body seemed ready to collapse.

Wouldn't do anyone the least bit of good dwelling on it though. Best keep moving. Keep killing kobolds where he saw them. Best die fighting, die on his feet in a way that would make his son proud.

Forward, then. Keep running.

The land was sloping upward. Growing harder and harder to make each step.

Maybe here was where he ought to stop. Turn, face the kobolds. Buy the others a moment, a few breaths more. Couldn't say as he ever forgot seeing the Axe sacrifice himself that way back on Thule. Couldn't say as he'd ever seen a braver man. It'd be good to be remembered like that.

And then the twisted trees gave way to scattered pines. Up the slope. Out of the cursed dale.

They'd made it?

He was still alive?

Pakkanen caught his arm, jerked him forward. "Don't stop. Keep moving. The others will catch up once we're clear."

Clear ... didn't sound possible, that. Still, he kept running. Few moments more. Right up until his legs gave out. He dropped to his knees in the snow, fell on his hands. Breathing hurt. It hurt like Hel herself was squeezing his lungs.

But it was a bit lighter here, outside the vale. Storm clouds still raged above, thundering. The occasional streak of lightning illuminating the sky.

Pakkanen dropped down beside him. "What happened back there?"

Good question, that. Couldn't say as Ecgtheow knew the

answer, though. Before he could catch his breath, the others came tromping out of the mist, winded all of them, even that giant Höfund.

Hervor doubled over, right hand on her knee, the other holding her runeblade limp. She looked up after a moment. "How did you find me?" she asked the giant. "How did you …"

Höfund spat some blood. He'd taken a slash to the face somewhere back there. "Been chasing you since I got your message all begging for help. Ain't been easy, neither. Come to this place and here I'm thinking I'd done wandered back into Jotunheim." Jotunheim? Hel's tits. The man was from there? Was he part jotunn? "Reckon you're damn lucky those villagers in Kalevala knew where you was headed."

Wudga frowned, glanced back in the direction of the dale. "We cannot linger here. The hiidet will pursue us, even in daylight. The sun doesn't shine bright enough here to drive them underground. Once night falls again, they'll attack in force."

Pretty much what Ecgtheow had expected. Which meant, he supposed he still might be having that heroic last stand in a few hours.

23

*S*tarkad jerked awake, suddenly aware of grass pressed hard against his face. He'd ... been having a nightmare. An awful vision of ... something. He felt weak, dizzy. Couldn't see well out of one eye and not at all out of the other.

"Gods," he mumbled.

A wind howled overhead, tangling his hair and tugging at his clothes. Must've been what woke him. He sat in a grassy meadow that stretched off in all directions, though rolling hills prevented him from seeing too far.

The tops of those hills were barren, weather-beaten, no doubt, and stripped of aught save rocks. Around them, though, a few trees dotted the countryside. No mist. No snows. Where the fuck was he?

He pushed himself to his feet, then swayed, unsteady and more than a bit woozy. Maybe he needed something to eat. A wash ... and a whole barrel of mead.

Still swaying, he stumbled off toward one of the hills. He should be able to get a better lay of the land from atop it. The wind just kept roaring around him, almost enough to

153

push him over. It would be worse up there by the rocks, but it still seemed his best shot at orienting himself.

As he drew nigh, though, the sound of rushing water reached him even over the unending gale. Water might mean fish, maybe people. It definitely meant a place to get a drink and clean himself up. He followed the sound around the base of the hill, and further to a stream. The waters flowed faster and faster as he followed them.

Until they ended in a giant waterfall that pitched off into open air. Starkad gaped. He stood on land, but that land seemed to be soaring through the sky. A sky that went on forever, save for other floating islands drifting around in it.

Dozens of falls pitched water from the islands endlessly, many pouring into rumbling storms beneath. Far below him —impossible to judge distance like this—a spiraling storm seemed to stretch for miles. A tempest big enough to swallow entire kingdoms.

Vertigo seized him as he looked down, sent the world spinning. Starkad backed away from the edge, pitched over backwards, and landed on his arse.

He was in the sky.

He was in the fucking sky.

And below him was only more sky. And above him. Just open air ... in all directions. The land a tiny afterthought, and himself an insect upon it.

"What the ...?" He couldn't swallow. Couldn't think. The scope of the world he found himself in defied his mind's grasp. "I ..."

A flood of nightmare visions flashed before his eyes. An instant of drowning and burning and tortures without end, all compressed into a moment. Starkad gasped, pressed his palms to his face, and crawled along the ground.

Another cascade of images rushed through his mind, nonsensical and horrifying.

Where was he? Why was this happening?

He ... Ogn?

You must find whatever spirit holds your soul here and confront it.

Afzal? How was the Serklander here?

An eagle cried above, circling over him. Eagle ... why the bird?

Confront it.

A spirit—a vaettr was tormenting him. And Afzal wanted him to confront it, to overcome it. Where was Ogn? Could she help him?

Again, the eagle's cry tore him from his musings. Starkad stared at the bird, which banked low, then soared off, back around the hill.

As good a direction as any—and far better than walking straight off the edge of the island. Starkad heaved himself up and trotted after the bird, eager to be as far from that vertigo-inspiring ledge as possible.

The eagle flew on, beyond the hills and over another meadow. Starkad panted, fatigued from chasing after it. Much more so than he ought to have been. His legs ached with a fire. His lungs burned. And he still couldn't quite see properly, like everything was viewed through a faint haze, a piece of glass that wasn't completely clean.

Still trying to catch his breath, he pushed on into the meadow. A black-haired woman was there, holding hand of a child, maybe five winters behind him. The woman turned, smiled at him.

"Starkad!" Hervor said. "There you are! We've been waiting all day, you know. Go on, Vikar, embrace your father."

The child scampered toward him. "Father!" The boy threw his arms around Starkad's legs and nigh bowled him over.

Awkwardly, Starkad patted him on the back of his head. His ... son? Of course. His son with Hervor: Vikar. A smile cracked his face, and he knelt, properly embracing the boy. "I had some things to take care of. But I'm here now. Here for both of you."

Hervor smiled again, rolled her eyes and chuckled. "Can't really stay vexed at you when you talk thus, now can I?"

"I'd hope not." He was laughing himself. Gods, when was the last time he was this happy? He couldn't even remember. Shit, he had a hard time remembering aught before this moment. Maybe because none of it mattered. Right now, he had all he'd ever need.

"Are we gonna make a bonfire tonight?" Vikar asked. "Are we gonna roast rabbits?"

Starkad nodded. "Of course we are. I just ... just have to catch them."

Oh ... wait. He shouldn't go. He shouldn't leave ...

He turned from the pair of them and started for the nearby woods. "Let me check the snares. I'll be back in an hour at the most."

"Best be," Hervor said, "or I'm coming looking for you."

No. No, he should stay here. Why was he walking away? That wasn't what he wanted to do.

"Starkad?"

He turned back.

A bird the size of a man screeched overhead, its enormous shadow looming over Hervor. The creature swooped down on Hervor. Only it wasn't a bird, though it had bird-like wings and talons. It had the head and breasts of a woman, twisted in a mask of grotesque rage. Its talons latched onto Vikar's shoulders, punching through flesh and spraying blood on Hervor.

The shieldmaiden bellowed and punched at the monster but had no weapons.

Nor did Starkad, though he was already running at the creature screaming. Vikar wailed, the bloodcurdling shriek of a child in agony.

A single beat of the creature's massive wings carried it aloft, high over Starkad's head. "No! Wait!"

The creature cast him a single, hate-filled glance, then swooped high over him, in the direction he'd come from. Starkad scrambled after it at a dead run, desperately chasing after its receding form. No matter how hard he pushed himself, still the flying monster easily outdistanced him.

It disappeared behind a hill, and Starkad bellowed, blundering on after it. Vikar! Vikar! His son!

Perhaps then, live the lives of three men ... and find victory. But not peace. Never peace ... never hope, never to sire children.

The words came unbidden to his mind, a memory almost lost. Almost buried.

No. It wasn't real. He refused to accept it. Roaring in rage, Starkad pushed harder, racing after the flying monster.

Never to sire children ...

Lies! That was not his life. His life was there, in the sky, bleeding out in the talons of the monster.

The flying creature turned about, flapping around over the open sky. Taunting him.

Starkad staggered to a halt at the very edge of the island, teeth grit and panting, chest heaving. He roared defiance at the monster holding his son. Roared until his throat was raw. Until his roar became a pitiful, wailing sob.

"Give him back!"

Vikar turned his face toward Starkad with agonizing slowness. His cheeks had turned to ash. His flesh began rapidly corroding away.

"Vikar!"

Never to sire children ...

A heavy gust swept over the monster. Starkad's son's body exploded into dust and billowed away in long, soul-crushing spirals, carried out over the eternal sky.

All coherent thought broke inside Starkad's mind. A terrible emptiness settled in.

Naught remained for him now. All had been taken by the dark.

He stared into the swirling tempest below. Naught but emptiness remained.

And he stepped off the island's edge.

Faster and faster he fell, until wind threatened to rip his clothes clean off his body. Until he passed into the storm below. A gale caught him and hurled him around in spiraling arcs. The winds battered him. Their roar deafened him.

Hail and ice particles stung his face. Lightning coursed before him, giving him a brief scent of burnt air, until the gale flung him far from that spot.

The elements beat and pummeled him, tore him to pieces.

But he cared naught. Let the wind carry him where it would.

24

From Ajatar's dale, they had pressed on. Hours more, until Hervor had finally let everyone stop. The crew had fallen into a fitful sleep, barely able to manage anyone on watch. A few hours of that, and they had to be on the move again. Couldn't afford to let the hiidet catch up. Besides, Starkad couldn't afford any delay.

And for days it went on like that, sleeping a few scant hours here and there. Until she felt she was walking in a dream. Like all of this had become some extended nightmare. Her eyes burned. Her feet were blistered and weeping blood inside her boots. Her wounds sapped what little strength might have otherwise remained to her.

Hardly anyone spoke at all. Fatigue tightened its grip around all of them. Even Wudga—who sometimes seemed more than human—appeared to have grown clumsy in his steps. As if each movement took a momentous effort of will. Hervor knew the feeling all too well.

The shaman trudged along beside her now.

"How much farther?" she rasped.

He paused, looked up at the sky. A hint of stars peeked

out behind a small gap in the rumbling storm clouds. "Not far now. We're nigh to the edge of Loude, Loviatar's kingdom. Once we cross through, we'll face the workings of her Art."

Odin's balls. In case they hadn't faced enough hardships with the hiidet. Hervor shook her head. "Then let's get it over with."

A few more hours they walked, and the mist ahead of her seemed to thicken, almost refusing to part before her torch. Hervor pressed forward, felt like the very air pushed back against her. Her ears popped and her head fogged up.

She turned to ask Pakkanen if he'd felt it—the shaman had vanished into the mist.

Hervor spun. No sign of anyone else. "Höfund?" She backed up. "Wudga? Ecgtheow?"

Oh, troll shit.

She twisted around again, waving the torch. Couldn't even say which way she was going anymore. It was like she'd blundered into another world. Loude, no doubt.

And then the mist broke away before her, parted and thinned clearer than she'd seen since coming into Pohjola. Beyond it lay a village, a few dozen huts by the look of it. The sky had turned pale green. The land beneath her seemed to twist and writhe like it was in pain. Thorns twice her size sprouted from the ground, bent around in crooked shapes that almost looked like men.

Hervor put a hand on Tyrfing's hilt. "Höfund!"

Moaning sounded from behind her and she spun. A hint of a face seemed to press against the air as if from the underside of a sheet. Many such faces, wailing on the wind. Pushing into the world and then vanishing without any sign they'd been there.

"Odin's balls ..."

Pulse pounding, Hervor advanced into the village, torch out before her. Hurt to hold it in her right hand, but she needed to keep her left free to draw Tyrfing. Odin alone knew what was going on in this place.

She stepped around a hut and faltered, gaping at the massive husk of a tree. She'd been so focused on the twisted village before, she'd barely noticed it towering above her, higher than any king's hall. Or maybe it hadn't been there a moment ago. Dozens of corpses hung from its branches, upside down.

The bodies swayed ever so slightly in the breeze. Turned, slowly. As they came around, their hollow eye sockets seemed to stare at her. Accuse her. Because they *knew*. All her crimes—the murders, the lies, the betrayals.

They knew them all.

And they called her to join them in the boughs. To take her rightful place alongside them, beyond the gates of Hel.

Hervor's feet started forward of their own accord. She knew where she belonged. There was no denying it. Urd had caught up with her at last.

The sky grew darker with each step she took.

Blue lightning cracked through the air.

Her feet kept plodding forward toward the tree of death. The dead called her. They welcomed her into their ranks.

Her heartbeat sounded in her ears like a drum. A drum whose rhythm had begun to slow. The time between each beat grew longer. Longer. Until soon, it would cease all together.

And still she walked forward.

The shadows coalesced before the tree. Seemed to form into a man, though not one of flesh. A cluster of twisted branches jutted from his back as he strode from the tree, arcing around him like the limbs of a spider. A mask of wood obscured his face and chitinous armor encased his legs, leaving bare only a scarred chest and abdomen from which more clawing branches jutted.

The manifested shadow growled at her in some foreign tongue, the guttural words reverberating inside her skull. As if on command, her legs gave out, and she fell to her knees. The torch slipped from her grasp. Her arms spread wide. Welcoming the end.

From behind itself, the tree warrior pulled a branch. The rod extended to become a sword, nigh as tall as she was, held in both of its hands as it stalked forward. The ground trembled in its wake. Its words beat down against her brain. Sapped all that remained of her will.

The end beckoned.

A roar sounded behind her. Distant. Far away. Meaningless next to the deafening cacophony of death's words.

For it was death that trod toward her, charging now. Sword raised.

Hervor tilted her head back, exposed her neck. Drew her final breath.

The sword descended.

Another blade halted its descent, the clang of metal on metal shattered the chorus in her mind and sent Hervor pitching over backward, suddenly in control of herself once more. Ecgtheow jumped over her prone form, swinging his blade down at the tree creature.

It parried. Hissed, its branches shuddering like snakes about to strike. Hervor jerked Tyrfing free of its sheath and thrust upward, through the creature's exposed abdomen.

The monster faltered, its blade falling limp to one side.

With a roar, Ecgtheow chopped into its neck. Black blood exploded out of the creature. Even as its corpse fell, though, it crumbled into ash and burnt up before Hervor's eyes.

Ecgtheow heaved, panting, shaking his head. "What the fuck?"

Hervor had no idea. She climbed to her feet, edging away from him. "Where are the others?"

"Can't rightly say. I was alone until I spotted you."

She swallowed. "Some kind of illusion ... Maybe they're here, we just all wandered in a daze."

"Right, well, you're welcome. Not that you overmuch deserve the saving. Just that I suppose Starkad's best chance is with you alive."

A resounding endorsement if she ever heard one. Ecgtheow clearly wasn't going to let this go, was he? The Arrow's Point had gotten to him, got him all turned around against her. And now he wasn't listening to aught she said on the matter. But if he kept bringing this up, sooner or later it would get back to Starkad.

And that she could not allow. No matter if she owed Ecgtheow ... no matter what, she couldn't let Starkad find out what she'd done to his friend Orvar. And that meant Ecgtheow couldn't make it back to tell him.

The thought soured her stomach. He'd just saved her life. But then again, he'd made it clear he'd turn on her as soon as Loviatar was dead. Which made him a fool—if he intended to betray her, he ought to have done without the warning.

"We have to find the others," she said.

"Indeed." He spat, and stalked away, forcing her to follow or risk being left alone again. That thought did not much appeal.

Beyond the tree, a sea of spikes rose up in the middle of the village. Thorns like the ones she'd seen before, except these had impaled corpses. Flayed corpses, their blood oozing down the giant spikes. A few of the dead sputtered, coughed, flailed, as if somehow yet alive against all rational possibility.

It wasn't real.

Hervor shut her eyes tight, shook her head.

Maybe none of this was real. Please, Odin, let none of it be real.

She opened her eyes, but the thorns and the moaning corpses lingered.

"Why is the sky green?" Ecgtheow asked.

As if that was the biggest fucking question about this hideous land. But indeed, even the vestiges of mist that wafted in had taken on a luminous green tinge. The very earth seemed to pulsate with every step she took.

The world itself wanted to reject this reality almost as much as Hervor did.

"Just keep moving," she mumbled. Given the damage to her voice, he probably couldn't have made out her words.

Nevertheless, he did press forward, following around a winding path between the impaled corpses.

"Hervor ..." one of the bodies called to her as she passed.

She grit her teeth, forced herself not to look. Eyes forward.

"Hervor ..."

"Hervor ..."

They were calling her. They, too, wanted to count her among their number. The damned calling out to their own.

Ecgtheow didn't react. Either didn't hear them, or was lost in his own waking nightmare. She locked her gaze on his shoulders, careful to not let it stir in the least. Not allow it to glimpse her periphery and the horrors begging her to join them.

Even as her mind's eye played it out, showed a thorn bending down for her. Waiting for her to thrust herself upon it. As if the torment it offered might somehow come as a relief from the unending agony and lies her life had become. It waited for her …

She ground her jaw until it felt like her teeth would crack open.

Ecgtheow had paused before a hut large enough to have housed a jarl's court. He glanced back at her. "Think Loviatar is in there?"

Hervor nodded, desperate to focus on aught other than suicide and eternal damnation. If she killed the witch-queen, maybe all this would end. Waiting for no invitation, she pushed past Ecgtheow and charged the hut. Kicked in the door and burst inside.

A woman screamed.

A great mass of people clad in furs and rough garb huddled around a fire pit, staring at her in obvious fear. No warriors among them, at least none with obvious weapons. Women, children, old men. All hiding here in some chief's place—hiding from her.

Her grip tightened around Tyrfing's hilt. It was hungering for blood. Feeding it the tree monster may have satisfied the curse, but it wanted more. She could feel it. It wanted these people. All of them.

Hel's frozen underworld.

She turned back to Ecgtheow, intent to tell him to back away. That they had to go before she did something she'd never live down.

A seven-foot tall man stepped out of the shadows and plowed into Ecgtheow, sending him flying out the door. Hervor dove to the side, barely avoiding being snared by his mighty hand. The man was coated in shadows, his form obscured, fluid even. He wore a helm that seemed like reindeer antlers, jutting out so far it almost scraped the rafters. He was clad in a bear-skin but no other obvious armor.

Twin battle-axes dropped into his hands and he bellowed, swinging with one and then the other.

Hervor threw herself sideways, rolled, and swept Tyrfing up just in time to block the descent of another of those axes. The man recoiled from the impact and she used his hesitation to lunge forward, sweep her runeblade at his arm.

The blade nicked the shadow man's forearm, but he jerked away, faster than a man of his size ought to be. He spun, leaping in the air and hurling one of the axes at her with his momentum.

Hervor yelped, leapt to the side, the axe soaring within a hairsbreadth of her face.

Already the warrior was charging her again, fighting with no regard for his own safety. Maybe because he wasn't even fucking real. Wasn't really alive so why should he care if he died?

Her, on the other hand ...

Hervor ducked, dodged, parried. Fell onto the defensive under the warrior's relentless attacks. A living man ought to have tired from swinging so violently about, but this warrior just kept flailing away like his weapon weighed no more than a feather.

Whatever it weighed, though, it was no runeblade.

Grunting as her foe came on again, Hervor brought Tyrfing up in a two-handed parry. Tyrfing slid up the haft of the axe and its blade caught on her crossbar. She jerked the blade down, slicing off all the warrior's fingers.

The axe tumbled from his bloody grasp and she whipped Tyrfing back around, burying it into the man's chest. He instantly exploded into ash and vanished into the air, even as Ecgtheow was blundering back into the hut.

Hervor shot him a glare. "You're late."

She looked back to the gathered villagers. They still clung to one another, not one of them had risen during the entire fight. They just stared at her, wide-eyed, as if she'd gone mist-mad.

Maybe they hadn't even seen the fight?

Either way, she ducked out of the hut, Ecgtheow on her heels. "I'm starting to think we can't find the others in this place. Maybe the thing to do is to push past here and try to regroup beyond the village."

Ecgtheow shrugged, then grunted assent.

With a last glance at the hut, Hervor trotted onward, eager to put the twisted village as far behind her as possible.

25

*R*umbling storm clouds billowed all around Starkad, battering him and stripping all sense from his mind and all hope from his soul. He barely noticed as that rumble gradually subsided. For the first time in an age, he wasn't falling, though he couldn't recall having hit aught either. He lay upon a rocky floor—a cavern, perhaps.

Only the barest flicker of light made it to him, far away and pathetic, a candle against the night. All around him, shadows danced and stretched, seeming thick as tar. Like a nest of serpents, those shadows crawled over Starkad, ensnaring and crushing his limbs, his chest, his throat.

Darkness pulled him under, into oblivion. He lay in the shadows, convulsing and pathetic. And after another age, he found the shadows had so saturated him, they no longer held him prisoner. He pushed himself up, blinked, and trembled with a rush of trepidation he could not explain, except to think he was not alone in the darkness.

Teeth grit, he gained his feet. The shadows were so thick, he couldn't make out much. Beside him, a veritable forest of skeletons lay piled up. A stack of bones taller than he was, as if hundreds of the slain had been left to rot in great heaps.

The thought left him queasy as he wandered through the caverns. Stalactites and stalagmites segmented off some paths and obstructed others, often coming together to form columns. More skeletons lay scattered about, broken and dusty.

He pressed on toward the distant, flickering lights far ahead. A few dozen candles, maybe? Torches, perhaps, or braziers if they lay farther than he judged. Either way, his only sign of the living.

Fire is life.

That much seemed to hold true in any world. The cavern opened up more ahead. Blundering forward, Starkad lurched to a sudden stop. The floor dropped away into a chasm that descended into unknown depths.

He sucked in a sharp breath and backed away, then followed a narrow ledge around the pit. Beyond this, the ground became even more uneven, forcing him to navigate rising and falling rock piles, while avoiding yet further drops.

In the far distance, a spire came into view. One of the flickering lights came from up there, in a high window. The others seemed spaced out along the top of the walls beneath that tower. Most like, they were braziers, then. Watch fires, of a sort, in this dark world.

Of a sudden, dark figures melted up out of the shadows, converging around him. Men and women with jet black hair and swarthy skin in varying shades of ashen gray.

One of them strode forward, chuckling, shaking his head. His long black hair stretched down over his bare, tattoo-marked chest. "Oh. I have thought to hunt for you, to tempt some mortal wretch to open the way to your world that I might feast upon your wilted soul. But it seems the twisted weavings of urd run thick with bitter irony and you fall back into the darkness that engendered your so-called glory."

Starkad reached for his blades over his shoulder, but none were to be had.

Something struck him from his blind side, cracking on his skull. He toppled to the ground, a flash of lights before his eye. "Who ...?" His speech was slurred and thick.

"You do not recognize me without Jorund's faltering host to contain me?" The svartalf chuckled. "Bring him."

Svartalfar heaved him up by his forearms and half-dragged him along, toward the fortress in the distance. Starkad struggled to make his mind work through the haze.

Jorund ... Jorund had been possessed by a svartalf ... Skafinn. So their leader here was the same one, and obviously quite vexed at Starkad forcing him back to his own world.

The fortress itself stretched up into the concealed reaches of this cavernous realm, the peak of its spire lost in shadow. The place put even the great works of the Old Kingdoms to shame. All of it was carved from black stones, jutting out at vicious angles that seemed apt to slice the air itself to ribbons. Jagged crenellations ringed the top, beyond which lay the braziers Starkad had seen from a distance.

A natural stone bridge spanned a crevice with no bottom in sight, offering the only ingress Starkad could see. A spiked iron gate five times his height closed off access to the main entrance. As the svartalfar drew nigh, though, the gate creaked upward, sliding into unseen recesses.

Even with his eye adjusted to the darkness, there was barely enough firelight to see inside the castle. The shadows here writhed like living things, coiling and flowing over every surface, dancing just out of reach of the few sconces that lined the inner walls.

Starkad swallowed, his head finally beginning to clear. There was something he had to do. Something needful for him to escape this place ... though from the look of this fortress, escape might no longer be an option.

Skafinn led the way through winding, maze-like corridors. The occasional glint of torchlight off metal made it seem like spikes or razors decorated the walls, ready to impale or shred any who drew too nigh. After long wandering, the corridor opened up into a great chamber lined by a series of columns on either side. Dark metal spikes jutted from each column in a web of blades and death. Farther up, barely visible, carved monstrosities of stone hung from the columns, leering down upon the hall.

Starkad could not make out the ceiling nor the walls through the darkness, which was broken only by a torch on every other column, and those shedding far less light than he'd have expected of the flames. As they trod down this hall, a raised dais came into view, drenched in shadow such that he could make out little of the occupant until they reached the foot of the steps.

The figure wore sharp-ridged armor of interlocking metal sheets unlike aught Starkad had ever seen. The edges of that armor looked like razors as well. The man's eyes held a faint luminescence—or perhaps an opalescence, glimmering in the darkness. The figure leaned forward, black hair hanging around the edges of his face, almost concealing his faint smirk.

"Starkad Eightarms ..."

"Volund?"

The great smith leaned back on his throne, his armor creaking ever so faintly. He spread his hands as if in a magnanimous gesture, a man welcoming a friend into his home. But Volund had no friends, so far as Starkad knew.

Starkad swallowed. Skafinn had not served Volund, last Starkad had heard. "What happened to Rathwith?"

Volund's smirk only deepened. "Wandering in exile, assuming naught has devoured his essence. If he yet survives the void, he no doubt struggles to hold on to the tattered remnants of his soul. Defeat ... comes with a hefty price, does it not, Eightarms?"

"And you are king here now?"

"A prince. Our people have not had a king in eons ..." But that might change. Volund didn't say it, but his ambition seemed to hang in the air. "I am, of course, bound by certain traditions, you know. And you did get my son to turn against his heritage ... While not altogether unplanned for, I cannot say I welcomed the betrayal."

Starkad kept his mouth shut. A pit opened in his stomach, a nameless fear of what he knew must come next.

Volund shifted again, almost seeming in pain. "I see you already understand where this is going."

Skafinn cracked Starkad between the shoulder blades. He dropped hard to the ground, slamming his knees on the stone and only half noticing as he tried to get his breath back. In the hidden recess of the ceiling, iron cranked above.

When Starkad managed to look up, a spiked metal chain was descending, nigh level with him now. Starkad tried to rise, but Skafinn drove him down with another blow. The svartalf wrapped the chain around Starkad's ankles and spikes the length of a finger joint punched through his flesh, scraping clear to his bones. He gasped in pain.

The creaking sounded again, and the chain jerked taut, pulling him upside down to hang from his ankles. Blood dribbled down his legs. Over his stomach. Dripped into his face and stung his eye.

Starkad grunted at the pain of it, then grit his teeth, refusing to give Volund the satisfaction of further crying out.

"Well," Volund said, now seeming to hang upside down from the ceiling. "Traditions being what they are ..."

The chain turned, ever so slightly, as Starkad struggled against it. As it twisted, he caught sight of Skafinn donning a clawed metal glove, the palm and back of the hand lined with knife blades. Starkad's captor stalked around until he stood before Starkad. Then he lunged forward, digging claws into Starkad's gut. The svartalf jerked his hand downward, tearing gouges from Starkad's belly up to his chest.

Now Starkad gasped once more, barely about to keep from crying out. He sucked in deep breaths. Blood poured over his face. Trickled into his nostrils. Obscured his vision.

Skafinn sneered, then placed a clawed finger at the bottom of Starkad's abdomen. With agonizing slowness, he dug the claw into Starkad's gut. Then he pulled slowly, ripping open a wide tear.

Starkad gave over any attempt not to scream. He *howled*. Skafinn dug his hand inside, wrapped it around Starkad's intestine, and slowly drew it out.

As Starkad's scream finally gave out—his breath spent— he heard cawing from the shadows above, like a raven sat upon one of the carved monsters.

Volund cocked his eye, a hint of a wry smile crossing his face. "That will be enough, Skafinn."

"My lord. I have only begun—"

"Enough." Volund rose from his throne and drifted toward Starkad, the shadows pooling and dancing around him like vile escorts.

Starkad gurgled, spat out his own blood. If Skafinn had

pierced his bowels he'd be in for a long, agonizing death. The thought settled in his mind, niggling him. Shouldn't ... shouldn't he have died already? Hadn't he wanted to die?

Volund limped down the stairs, supporting himself on a metal staff topped with two curving, spiked fork tines. "Leave us."

Skafinn sputtered in almost human indignation.

"*Leave* us." Volund's tone brooked no further discussion and, almost at once, Skafinn and his warriors turned and fled the throne room.

Starkad gasped again, finding it hard to even stay conscious.

Volund stalked past him, circling once, limping with every step. He never took his gleaming eyes off Starkad, but Starkad couldn't begin to guess what went on behind them. Finally, the smith-turned-prince pressed on and touched something on a column. The chain cranked once more, this time lowering Starkad back to the floor.

Starkad collapsed in a heap, unable to even form a coherent thought, much less speak.

"Traditions ..." Volund murmured. "Ah, burdensome at times. We are left with reputations to maintain, you see."

Starkad groaned.

Volund knelt then. The prince began unwrapping the chain from Starkad's ankles. As each spike popped from his flesh, Starkad winced at the fresh jolts of pain.

"Well ... traditions being fulfilled, I fear the time has come to bid you farewell, my friend." Volund pulled the last of the chain away from Starkad's legs.

Starkad rolled over just a hair, teeth grit against the pain of even that much moving. Then, gingerly, cringing at the pain, he eased his intestine back inside his belly. "Kill me ...?"

"Oh ... I rather think your soul can take a bit more. It is strong—at least it was before you found yourself drawn into the Spirit Realm. Not so much remains of it now. When it breaks, one or another of those you call vaettir will feast upon it and drink in glorious power. But not myself, Eightarms. I will send you on your way."

"I c-can't walk ..."

Volund sneered. "Really. You will bemoan your pain to *me*? Whine, like a dog over the agony of walking? Do you think I, of all people, will offer you sympathy? Has Odin so badly mischosen his would-be emissary?" The prince stood, leaning on his staff a moment. Then he let it clatter to the floor beside Starkad. "Get up, you simpering dotard. Show me your soul is worth more than a feast."

Dotard? Fuck him. Starkad growled. Fuck the prince and all the godsdamned svartalfar and Odin too.

"Odin bought your power, drew it from this very world. It cost you ... but then it cost him as well. Was it worth the price?"

Starkad sucked in deep breaths. He lunged for the staff and wrapped one hand around it. Metal scraped on stone as he pulled it vertical. Then he yanked himself to his knees, other hand grabbing the staff as well. His power ... came from Svartalfheim. Long life ... and stamina beyond that of other men. Maybe he'd never eaten the fruit of Yggdrasil ... but he was still Starkad fucking Eightarms.

Growling, he pulled himself to his feet. The pain in his ankles, the agony in his gut, they dimmed, fueling rather than impeding his rage. "My power ..."

"Yes ... Come." Volund limped away, between two columns toward a side wall of the chamber.

Leaning on the staff, Starkad pulled himself on after the svartalf. "I ... ought to ... kill you."

Volund cast a sneer his way, one eyebrow raised. He said naught, nor perhaps needed to. A silent reminder that here, he had become a prince. That, if Starkad had gained a drop of strength from the World of Dark, Volund had bathed in it. Besides, in his own way, maybe Volund was helping him.

And so Starkad limped and shambled after the prince. Volund led him to an archway filled with mist so thick Starkad could not see half a foot into it. "Reality is not quite what humans think it. Hmm ... It is tenuous and mercurial, among other things. Human logic and reason applies very little once you move beyond the human realm—if even there."

And the way forward lay through the mist. And why not ... beyond must lay Niflheim itself. The World of Mist. The land of Hel. And if he was to pass through this Spirit Realm to ... confront his nightmares, his chance must lay within.

He drew a deep breath, then started forward, still leaning on the staff.

"Eightarms," Volund said.

Starkad looked back at him.

"Pain and suffering are the crucibles through which greatness is forged. I would know ..."

It was hard to say whether he ought to hate the svartalf or thank him. Instead, Starkad just offered him a nod.

Then he trudged into the mist.

26

*A*s Hervor had hoped, beyond the edge of the village, the others had regrouped. None had much wished to discuss what they'd seen within, leaving her to imagine they had each faced their own nightmares. Maybe Loviatar was playing with their minds. If so, it gave Hervor all the more reason to want the witch dead.

The hills gave way to mountains, and they pushed on until exhaustion drove them to collapse. And as soon as they were able, they were up again, pressing ever deeper. They had finally crossed beyond the storms and here, the sky swirled in a dance of color and light more miraculous than even what she'd seen on Thule.

"Glorious," Höfund mumbled.

Hervor felt too fatigued to even bother answering.

And then, as they crested the peak of another mountain, it came into view. At first, she took it for an obelisk the height of a mountain. But the alabaster column twisted and wound about itself. Even from here, she could see its surface seemed gnarled with knots. The tip of it pierced the clouds and scraped the sky beneath the North Star.

"Odin be praised ..." Ecgtheow said.

"What is that?" Hervor asked, unable to swallow.

Pakkanen huffed up beside her, shook his head while he caught his breath, before finally staring up at the column. "Never thought ... I'd see it ... the World Pillar. Some say ... it is a root of the World Tree, connecting Midgard to the heavens above."

World Tree? Odin's magnificent balls! "I ..." She had no idea what she even wanted to say. Ecgtheow was right, praise Odin. Praise all the Aesir. She squinted at the pillar. It grew out of a valley. Just above the mist, some construction rimmed its surface, a balcony running around it.

"You see it, don't you?" Pakkanen said. "Loviatar's palace."

She had built *onto* the World Pillar? The very thought seemed audacious to the point of blasphemy, as if she proclaimed herself a goddess above the land.

"Reckon that's who you want dead," Höfund said. "Don't look like a weak one, though, whoever built that place. Ain't gonna be easy to take the fight there."

Hervor sniffed, rubbed the chill from her cheeks. "Never thought it would be."

She started down the mountain slope.

THE SHEER SCOPE of the World Pillar boggled the mind and defied imagination. From the mountain peak, it had seemed massive. Now, approaching its base, no word seemed sufficient to sum up its magnitude. Hervor was an insect beneath an endless cliff.

Unable to focus on the scope of the pillar itself, she

instead locked her gaze on the balcony that rimmed it. A walkway spiraled around the root, rising up to the balcony itself, which stood maybe thirty feet in the air. It might have been wood, but it gleamed like polished stone in the same alabaster color as the root itself.

What she hadn't seen from the peak, though, was the campfires scattered around the base of the root, nor the huts from which now poured a small army of tattooed warriors. These people wore no clothes other than animal skins, with the skulls of bears or reindeer as masks. They bore crude spears and axes, looking no less horrifying for having weapons made from bone or rock.

It was not the warriors circling their small party that drew her eye, however. From some room beyond the balcony a woman had emerged, drawn up to the rail and stared down at them. Stared eyelessly, as it were. Where her eyes ought to have been rested only pools of inky blackness. Dark hair billowed about her, made her seem almost radiant in the night, especially against the gleaming backdrop of the World Pillar. Maybe Loviatar would have been beautiful despite her missing eyes.

Maybe, if Hervor weren't so intent on killing the woman high above her, staring down. Seeming to look right into Hervor's soul. Naught good ever came from sorcery or witchcraft, if there was even a difference between the two. The whole world would be better off if every worker of the Art just dropped dead.

For now, Hervor would have to settle for ending just one of them. Meeting the witch's gaze, she slid Tyrfing free of its sheath. "Come down and face us, witch, and your people may yet live."

Hard to say whether the savages understood her words,

though they did hoot and brandish their weapons when Hervor addressed their queen. Either way, Loviatar spoke to her people in some strange tongue, her words lilting and discordant.

And those words seemed to break a dam holding back the savages. Warriors burst forward in a wave, screaming high-pitched war cries and flailing their weapons with enough ferocity to make up for any lack of discipline. Almost enough.

"Take them," Hervor rasped to the others. "Clear a path to the witch!"

A warrior jabbed at her with a spear. Hervor jerked out of the way, cleaved through the haft of his weapon and whipped Tyrfing back around to tear through his jaw. The man fell screaming, hands over his split face. Probably didn't even realize he was already dead.

Hervor stepped around him, cut down another man.

Höfund charged past her, shoulder-slammed a warrior woman, and buried his axe into the sternum of a man. The others crashed into the army of savages, more than occupying them.

Hervor broke into a run, dashing for the walkway that led up to that balcony. Maybe the crew could hold off the warriors long enough for her to reach the top. There was a troll-sized serving of the fuckers, though, and none of her crew were Starkad, able to fight off a dozen men at once.

So she'd best be fast about this.

Running so hard she almost didn't see the shimmer flying through the air. At the last moment, she twisted, tried to dodge. The creature impacted her in the chest and sent her sprawling in the snow. Its momentum carried her away several feet, the hiisi atop her like she was a sled.

She lost her torch but just managed to hold on to the runeblade.

The creature bellowed a hideous croak at her, reared back and yanked at her mail with both claws. Then it bit down, rending metal links with its teeth. She flailed as it jerked its claws apart, shredding her armor and leaving naught but leather padding to protect her.

Hervor jerked her fist up, punched it in the throat. Even as it fell backward, one of its claws slashed into her chest, shredding leather and tearing deep into her left breast. She shrieked in pain, jerked Tyrfing up and drove the runeblade through the hiisi's eye, coating her hand in gore.

Hand to her chest, she yanked the blade free.

Turned. More hiidet were leaping atop her crew, laying into them. Nowhere nigh to the numbers they'd faced in Ajatar's dale, but too many. She glanced back at the walkway. The path was clear, but if she left her people to fend for themselves ... she might have no allies to come back to.

Then again, they were all like to be dead before the next sunrise. She had to finish Loviatar to save Starkad. Make all this mean *something*.

With a gasp of pain and frustration, she grabbed up her torch and blundered forward again. The snow was lighter on the walkway and her footfalls echoed on the wood as she raced upward. A long run, round and round the massive pillar.

Panting, she caught her breath by the rail for a heartbeat or two, then plodded on. She had to do this. She had to get it done. Naught else mattered until the witch-queen was dead.

Her legs ached. Her feet kept trying to turn over. As she circled round, more sounds of battle came from below. Screams of pain. Men and women dying. Shrieking croaks from the hiidet.

Don't look.

She couldn't afford to take her attention from the task at hand. Just keep running. Ribs were aching. Arm burning beneath the bandage. Just keep moving ...

She rounded the next bend.

The witch turned to her, as if able to see despite having no eyes. Looked right at Hervor. Hervor fell short, panting. Maybe she should have said something, but naught came to mind.

And then Loviatar stepped backward, disappearing into a building built up against the pillar's side. The edge of the doorway bore an elaborately carved relief, like Loviatar had indeed intended this place as a palace on the very ends of the world.

Beyond lay darkness, so Hervor strode forward slowly, torch out before her. "There is no escape, witch!"

Careful, watching for the shimmer of hiidet, Hervor strode inside. The witch stood before the edge of the pillar itself, hand on its surface, mumbling something under her breath.

As Hervor entered, the witch turned, stared right at her. "It is as you *fear* ..."

Her voice hit Hervor like a blow to the gut. Hervor stumbled forward, Tyrfing's point dropping low and scraping the wooden floor, leaving a scar in it. Hervor opened her mouth, but no sound came out. Her head was filled with mist. Everything around her swayed and spun like the deck of a ship. She stumbled a few steps forward.

"You are a pestilence upon all who know you."

Loviatar's words carved through her brain, a searing blade driven through her skull. Hervor staggered, dropped to one knee. She retched out rotten, black oil like the blood of the hiidet. It poured from her mouth, from her nose, from her ears. Her eyes wept the viscous, toxic fluid.

"You are corruption. A disease that spreads rot across all the land."

The sound of those words drowned out the noise of battle, of everything, save Hervor's own retching. Fits of coughing seized her and she spit out blood. Chills ravaged her body, drove her to the ground where she collapsed into the mix of her own vomit and toxins she spewed out with it.

"You touch darkness and, now, it consumes you."

Spasms shot through her limbs and sent her convulsing onto her back. Rolling around in the putrid filth she'd spread over the room. Her muscles seized up so tight they sent her head banging against the floor. White lights filled her vision.

"*I* touched the dark." A male voice. A hand on her shoulder. "Focus on why you are here. Your own mind makes her curses more real. You do the witch's work for her."

Hervor blinked the lights away. Wudga knelt beside her, one hand on her, the other clutching his blade.

Loviatar was there, too, sneering at him. "You think you know the dark?" The witch leaned back, put her hand against the root once again. And it folded around her, became a gaping void of utter blackness broken only by starlight. The witch stepped into that abyss and vanished.

Hervor fell back on the floor.

Everything went dark.

"Wake." Someone shaking her. Forcing her to open eyes that burned and did not want to see aught.

Hervor cracked her eyelids. Wudga was still kneeling over her. He gently slapped her cheek, then rose and moved to examine the pillar where Loviatar had disappeared. All at once, he backed away, shaking his head and frowning.

"She has gone," Pakkanen said.

Hervor turned to see the shaman standing in the doorway, clutching a wound on his side. Clearly in pain.

"The World Tree binds our world and the Otherworlds," the shaman said, then stepped aside to allow the others inside.

Höfund entered, bearing a half dozen cuts and scrapes, the deepest a long line on his back, dribbling blood over the floor. Ecgtheow followed him, looking even worse. Kustaa had his share of wounds too, though his face looked more angry than pained.

Hervor pushed herself up, then spit out the foul taste in her mouth. Had the witch actually infected her with some rot, or was that all in her head? She rubbed the back of her hand against her mouth. "What does that mean, Pakkanen?"

The shaman now examined the root where the witch had fled. "The pillar is a root of the great tree and thus connects it to other realms. I believe she fled into Tuonela, the Land of the Dead."

"How do we follow?" Hervor asked.

Pakkanen shook his head. "A shaman might undertake deep meditation to go there in spirit, but to travel there bodily as Loviatar has done ... I had not thought it possible. Certainly, I have no such powers at my disposal."

Wonderful. "Wudga?"

"No. A spirit journey—some kind of astral projection— is our only option now, assuming Pakkanen can bring us along for such a sojourn."

So not even Volund's son could do what Loviatar had.

Hervor shook her head. Still felt like it was full of cobwebs and poison. "We've no choice, then. Take us on the spirit journey. Whatever it takes, send us after her."

The shaman grimaced, shut his eyes a moment. "I can try to bring you along on such a vision quest, but it will take a lot out of me ... and of you. Your bodies will remain here, helpless, while your souls become untethered. What happens to you ... on the other side ... it will be real. Maybe more real than this world."

What did that even mean? Hervor worked her jaw, uncertain what to say to that. Finally, she grunted. "Whatever it takes."

Höfund spat, folded his arms and leaned against the wall. "Ain't much for spirits, me. Reckon I'll stay here and keep watch against any more of 'em showing up while you're sleeping."

"It is ... best that someone remain. Someone who could protect our bodies. If aught should befall them in the Mortal Realm, our souls would have naught to return to."

Odin's balls. This plan seemed drawn right up from mist-madness. Of course, if Hervor let on about that for even a moment, who knew how many others might back out. She needed them to take on Loviatar. So she nodded, face as impassive as she could manage.

Pakkanen set about tracing a circle inside the chamber, smearing his hands in blood from the numerous wounds Hervor's crew had suffered, the shaman himself included. Then came those awful runes, sigils that made Hervor's head hurt to even look upon.

Next, the shaman set torches in a ring around the circle, and beside them, bowls with some herb he pulled from his satchel, burning, casting a sickly-sweet smoke into the air. Finally, the last bowl in place and smoldering, he looked up, staring right at her. His eyes were bloodshot, but maybe that was just exhaustion. "Those who would journey must sit within the circle." The shaman himself stepped inside, carefully avoiding smudging the blood paintings. He sat just beyond the inner ring, holding a waterskin.

This was it. This was the moment she left all sense behind and embarked on quite possibly the most mist-mad trek she'd ever made—and that was saying something. Last chance to turn back …

Hervor took a long step over the painted circle, then sat down beside Pakkanen, legs folded beneath herself just like the shaman. She looked to Wudga, who followed her, taking a place beside her.

Ecgtheow groaned, glanced about, then shook his head and sat down beside Wudga.

Finally, Kustaa spat. Grumbled something under his breath. And joined them.

Pakkanen took a draught from the skin—probably not water—then passed it to Hervor.

Odin's thrice-damned freezing balls. This was starting to look an awful lot like how things had started with Gylfi, back when … when that *thing* had … Hervor couldn't quite force down the lump in her throat.

"Drink," Pakkanen said.

Fuck.

The ash-wife and her companion … They had …

"You must drink."

Walk … into the gates of Hel. Hervor took a swig. Smoky, acrid stuff stung her throat as it went down. The herb smoke had already made things hazy. The moment she drank, the room began to sway.

Coughing, she passed the skin on to Wudga. Didn't even see if he'd drunk it.

Everything was spinning. Going dark.
She shut her eyes.
Pakkanen had begun chanting or singing or ...
Everything faded into swirling shadows.
And she was lost.

PART III

Tuonela

27

*H*ervor opened her eyes. She still sat on the floor, in the circle, along with the others, but things had changed. Color and light had bled out of the world, leaving her reality a miasma of cool shadows. The torches around the circle, their flames, they had become ethereal reflections. Höfund, too, had turned translucent and wispy, barely visible at all. Like looking at him through a sheet of ice, and the fires were on his side of it.

The others in the circle, though, they seemed distinct, Kustaa's form becoming clearer even as she looked at him.

Pakkanen stood, his motion leaving faint afterimages in the shadows flickering around him. "Behold Tuonela."

Hervor groaned, pulled herself to her feet, followed shortly by the others. It was the same room, yes, but twisted. The angles were wrong, like a garment wrinkled. And everything seemed so dark.

She made her way out onto the balcony. The landscape before her was even more twisted. The same, but ever-so-slightly wrong. Shifted into shadow ... "The Otherworld."

"One of them," Pakkanen said. He pointed up at the sky.

The brilliant lights from before had been replaced by a dark sky suffused with starlight and a faint iridescent shimmer in the distance. If she squinted, she could almost fancy a bright crystal moon glittered among that shimmer.

"We're in the land of the dead?" she asked.

Pakkanen leaned on the rail, frowning at something down below. Hervor followed his gaze. Figures moved there, shadowy but clearly real. Clad in animal-skull helms and skins. The same warriors they had slain to reach Loviatar. Dead warriors. Ghosts …

"No shaman truly knows how far Tounela reaches or what lies beyond. Just that the dead go farther than we can ever see, and the vaettir come from a realm farther still beyond—the Spirit Realm, some call it. Everything beyond our realm, shades and spirits alike, they are made of hatred and lies. They would happily feast upon our souls. And by coming here, we cast ourselves upon their very tables."

"We are just on the other side of the Veil." Wudga's voice came from right behind her. "The farther we go from the Mortal Realm, the less reality resembles what we know. We should not dawdle in this place. Sooner or later, something will know we have come."

Hervor glanced back to see Ecgtheow and Kustaa exchange worried-looking glances. Everyone was waiting for her. She had made herself captain of this crew, and now they waited on her order. "She cannot have gone far. Stick together and look for the witch's trail."

"We ought to avoid the shades of those we have slain," Pakkanen said. "I will try to pick up Loviatar's trail while avoiding her … fallen minions."

Indeed.

IN THIS SPECTRAL REALITY, Tyrfing's ethereal fires had become an all too real blaze, roaring and crackling, casting more heat and light than a torch. Despite Pakkanen's attempts to avoid the shades, two of the fallen had beset Hervor.

The flames that sprang up upon her drawing the runeblade had shocked her almost as much as it seemed to shock the pair of shades. When she had struck one, it had burst into blue flames, flailing as it turned to smoldering ash. Tyrfing made short work of the other as well.

Hervor could get used to that. Except that the runeblade moved with a perilous will here, seemed almost to wield her. And now, as it blazed in her hand, she felt it drawing closer to Pakkanen.

With her jaw clenched against the pressure, she forced the blade back to her side.

The shaman wandered this place with glazed eyes, reading signs on the wind or ripples in the land, somehow following a trail that seemed nonsensical to Hervor.

"Sheathe the blade," Wudga said.

"What?" Hervor glanced up only to see Tyrfing had risen once more, edged its way closer to Pakkanen's open back. Damn. She grabbed her scabbard. As she slid the tip inside, the flames winked out, allowing her to drive the sword all the way in.

"Many things change in the Penumbra," Wudga said.

"Penumbra? I thought this was Tuonela."

"The Penumbra is the nearest part of the Astral Realm, what Kvenlanders call Tuonela. Names for that which we barely understand. This is a shadow of our world. And it grows darker the farther from home we tread."

Hervor rubbed her arms. The place lacked the biting cold of the real world, instead seeming caught in a perpetual chill that pierced through furs as if they weren't even there. "But *you* understand. You learned from your father."

Wudga frowned. "You believe even Volund understands the intricacies of creation? That seems ... unlikely."

So even a svartalf, a being tied to an Otherworld, still didn't have all the answers. She wasn't sure if that should comfort or terrify her. Either way, she fell silent. Words seemed foreign here, an intrusion against the natural order.

Pakkanen mumbled under his breath as they walked, ever glancing this way or that, sometimes straight up into the sky. The landscape grew more perilous as he led them out of the valley and into a mountain pass.

A quarter hour beyond this they reached a raging river, its waters dark, nigh to black, surging and coursing over rocks. It cut through the mountains like a blade, severed a peak in half in a way that defied reason.

"Fuck me," Ecgtheow said.

"The dead rivers divide the transitory lands of Tuonela. Our quarry has passed this and so must we."

"Swim that?" Hervor asked.

Pakkanen gasped and stared at her with eyes wide. "Set foot in there and you will never surface again—at least not as any living being we would recognize." He shook his head, glancing back to the river and scanning for something. "There must be ... There." He pointed far upriver.

A small boat was making its way downstream, guided by a black shrouded figure at the back of it. Just looking at the boat made Hervor's stomach go queasy, though she couldn't have said why. Maybe ... maybe because whatever operated this ferry was clearly no living person. If it ever had been.

"She's coming ..." Pakkanen said. "She must take us for dead."

"Shouldn't be hard," Ecgtheow said. "Most of us are more than halfway there."

Pakkanen stepped forward, to the river's edge. "Show no sign of life, no sudden moves, no flicker of emotion. We are the lost ones now."

Hervor let her face go slack—an effort, given the pounding of her heart.

The boat drew up close, then scraped onto the bank. Pakkanen was right about the ferryman being female, though her face was completely concealed beneath the cowl of her tattered shroud.

"Would you cross ..." Her voice was a whisper on the wind, hollow and foul.

"We would cross," Pakkanen said, as though it mattered to him naught at all.

"Pay ..."

The dead wanted money? Hervor started to shrug, then fought down the urge in case it might give her away. Instead, she simply pulled a silver coin from a pouch at her side and handed it out toward the woman. The creature reached out a spiny, bandage-wrapped hand and caught Hervor's wrist.

"A taste of your soul ... Given freely."

Caught in the woman's grasp, Hervor could barely move. Despite the creature's frail appearance, her grip seemed ready to crush the bones in Hervor's hand. The coin tumbled from her limp fingers and pitched into the river with a tiny splash.

A piece of her soul? What would that even mean? She wanted to look to Pakkanen, to ask his advice. To ask Wudga.

Maybe to just refuse.

Show no emotion, he had said. Be dead.

And was this how the dead paid their debts? Siphoning

off pieces of themselves until naught remained? Maybe that was why Pakkanen had warned to show no emotion. Because the dead lost such things one wretched bargain at a time.

"Take it," she rasped, trying to keep fear or aught else from her voice.

The shrouded woman leaned forward, seemed to suck air in toward her. An icy chill seeped up Hervor's arm and she could almost feel the warmth being drawn out into the ferryman's grasp. A tremble seized her, a shudder she could not quite fight down.

She clenched her teeth, struggled not to cry out as something deep inside bled out.

Visions flickered past her mind. Training with Gunther, learning the sword. Playing as a child, running and swimming. Laughing with Grandfather. Brawling.

Images that faded almost as quick as they'd come.

And she couldn't even remember what she'd just seen, what she'd been thinking of.

Without warning, the ferryman released her grip and Hervor wobbled, dropped to one knee. "You may board."

Get up. She had to get up. A profound chill had gripped her tight inside, wrapped around her guts. Get up.

She rose, a little wobbly. Maybe it hadn't been so bad. Who needed a soul, anyway?

Hervor stepped onto the boat and settled down at the front of it.

28

*T*he sharp wind swept down from snow-covered peaks rising out of the mist. Its bitter chill left Starkad shivering, frosting his beard and slowing his already painful steps. The dark metal staff Volund had given him had grown so cold merely grasping it had turned his fingers numb. But if Starkad cast it aside, he wasn't sure he could keep going.

The mist here was so thick he could make out less than ten feet in front of him, though he could still see the shadows of towering mountains stretching out across the horizon. The land of Hel, indeed. More frozen, more dire, and more endless than even the wastes of Jotunheim.

And the mist here was worse than on Midgard, moving and swirling about him, watching his steps and judging him damned for his crimes. Hard to say over the howling wind, but he'd have almost sworn the mist whispered in his ears, taunted him with empty promises and far from empty threats. It niggled at his soul and flitted away his memories, making it doubly hard to keep in focus his goal.

Someone ... Afzal ... had told him. He needed to find her. To confront her ...

Who?

Ogn.

Ogn, who took her own life in despair after Starkad killed her jotunn lover. Ogn, who'd become ... something that ought not to have been her urd. He'd damned her, too, just like all others who came nigh to his side. Just like ... someone else. There was someone he was meant to remember through all this.

Dark hair ... battle scars. Fierce ...

But far away, like a dream. A memory slipping from his grasp, fading into the mist, never to return.

All of Starkad would soon be lost. Unless he ... found Ogn. Saved her ... or himself.

Snow crunched under his heels as he trudged on, often sinking up to his shins. Below that, the snow was packed so tightly he could actually manage to stay atop it. Beaten down by its own weight, like Starkad.

Odin. The Ás king had stolen Starkad's power from the Dark. Made him ... Otherworldly ...

Now he wandered those worlds ... dreaming? Had Afzal said that?

The murmuring of a river rose up, reaching him even over the bitter cries of the wind and the maddening whispers of the mist. Water running and ... blades clinking together almost as in battle, though muted, and he heard no screams. Battle always came with screams. Pain and death—friends, now, to Starkad, for he knew them better than he knew any living soul. The few memories the mists could not touch.

Leaning on the staff, he pushed on through the mist, and

the crash of metal grew louder. Until he came to a river, swift and wide, icy, but unfrozen. Shadows swept by beneath the surface. Ice under the water? That didn't make sense. And ... He leaned forward to peer deeper. Not ice, exactly. Shards of frozen metal like knives, an endless stretch of them pulled along in the current, clanking together and apart.

Anyone fool enough to wade into the river would be impaled and shredded before he could draw a single breath.

A sudden gale swept across the waters, rippling them, and sending Starkad stumbling backward, his clothes billowing up around him. The wind blew the thickest of the mist downstream, revealing the far bank.

On that bank stood a figure, beckoning to him.

Starkad squinted his eye, barely able to make out the man. He didn't see so well these days. Was that ... Vikar?

His brother, waiting for him. Calling him closer. Urging him on to the far shore.

The chance to rejoin his brother after so long ... maybe that was what Starkad sought here. Maybe it was what he needed to finally find peace. He took another step toward the river, but hesitated. Those knives would tear him to pieces long before he could reach Vikar.

His brother waved again, pointing upstream. Behind him, shades moved in and out of the mist, too far away and too indistinct for Starkad to identify. And yet, he felt he knew them. That they too waited for him on the far side. That if he could but cross, he might, at last, find an end to his wanderings and his misery.

Vikar started off upstream, still beckoning.

Starkad grunted. "Wait ..." He couldn't afford to lose his brother. Not now. Not when he was so close.

He tromped through the snows, struggling to keep up with Vikar's faster stride. Starkad's legs felt like lead weights. His ankles had become frozen and weak. His body was ready to collapse. But Vikar, he just kept going, forcing Starkad to push himself, even as he stumbled.

Through the mists up ahead, something glittered like gold. A covered bridge rose up, colossal such that the tallest jotunn could have passed through without coming close to the roof. That roof itself was thatched with golden sheets covered in frost. The workmanship here defied understanding. Who could have wrought such a thing over the perilous river?

And why?

Vikar disappeared around the far side of the bridge, forcing Starkad to press on, until he could peer through the opening. His brother was now just a shadow in the distance, beyond the darkened tunnel before him. Scattered windows in the upper reaches of the bridge let in a crisscross of light beams, hardly enough to cast aside the shadows.

The mist itself drifted over the floor, thin, but enough to further obscure passage.

"Come to me ..." Vikar's voice carried on the mist, drifting to Starkad even from the vast distance between them.

Starkad swallowed. Yes ... he needed to cross. He needed to join those on the other side, those waiting for him. His staff clanked loudly as he took his first faltering step onto the bridge. It seemed to lengthen and deepen before him, reality warping with each successive foot he passed.

He was drawing closer, yes, but slowly, and Vikar still but a shadow.

"Beyond here lie the gates ..." Again, the voice whispered

along the ground, echoing out of the mist and ringing in Starkad's ears.

The gates. The gates ...

"Step beyond the gates of Hel and join me in eternity ..."

Yes. That was the right thing to do. The time had come to stop fighting. Starkad limped forward, staff grating on stone as he pulled himself along. He was almost done. Almost finished with everything. Rest was but a few steps more.

A raven's caw rang out from one of those high windows. The bird fluttered down and landed upon the head of Starkad's staff.

"Come to me ... walk through the gates of Hel ..." Vikar's voice had grown more urgent. Desperate, even.

Starkad took another step toward his brother. He had to get to him. He couldn't leave his little brother alone ...

The raven cawed again, spread its wings wide, and then took off, flying out the back side of the bridge, the way Starkad had come in. The bird? Why did he feel like it mattered? Why would a bird matter?

"Come to me ... Do not turn from the gates ... Do not falter ..."

Starkad glanced back at his brother's form, now a mere silhouette in the mist. "I ..."

The raven's cry echoed through the bridge, calling him back. The head of Starkad's staff had become a copy of that raven, staring at him. What did it mean? Hadn't he seen this before? The bird had helped him escape from ... something.

He needed to catch it, see what it wanted. Grunting, he turned to chase after the raven, his steps growing faster as he did so. The weight holding his legs diminished, ever so slightly.

"Come back ..."

Starkad glanced over his shoulder as he reached the end of the bridge. No sign remained of Vikar. Shit. He'd just find the raven first, then double back and get his brother.

He should get his brother ... Except it felt like he couldn't. Why wouldn't he be able to reach him?

Dammit. Starkad groaned and shambled back into the snow. "Bird!"

Another cry, in the distance.

Starkad followed it, wandering into a mist that grew thicker and thicker with each passing step. So dense he could not make out his hand in front of his face.

"Bird!"

Again, the shrill cry, this time off to his right.

Starkad turned toward it, shuffling on.

The land grew darker, as if the sun was setting too rapidly, though Starkad had seen no sun in the sky. Finally, as he drew on, the mist began to thin, until it too dissipated into naught. Color bled out of the world, leaving him in profound darkness.

The raven's caw echoed again, beckoning him onward. The snow gave way to solid rock beneath his feet, black as night. He was looking for something.

The thought didn't quite want to form in his mind. A general disquiet settled upon him, as if he had forgotten something of dire urgency. Or, perhaps, as if that something had been drained from his mind, siphoned away by some unseen force. The all-pervasive darkness here had a different quality than that he'd witnessed in Svartalfheim.

The land beneath him ebbed and flowed like jelly, itself seeming uncertain what shape it desired. Starkad groaned.

There was something to do. Someone he was meant to confront ...

But it all seemed so very far away.

And though he could not name what went missing, he felt sure more and more of himself bled away by the moment. A sudden realization settled upon him, a certainty that the world itself was hungry—and it was slowly devouring all he was.

But then, after all the years of wandering, of suffering, he found he almost welcomed the void.

29

The black river streamed by, flowing swiftly even as the boat eased along at a gentle drift. Something about that seemed off to Ecgtheow. He'd have otherwise supposed the boat ought to move at about the same speed as the current, but then again, he couldn't say as many things worked the way they ought to in this place.

And there was Hervor, sitting up in the bow, grim-faced and battered as the rest of them, but otherwise not much changed. Except for having bartered off a bit of her soul. Ecgtheow didn't suppose she'd had that much to begin with, but still. He'd have expected some sign, some indication the shieldmaiden had lost something precious.

The woman just kept staring at the waters, though, saying naught.

Until the boat scraped up on the opposite bank, far downstream from where they'd boarded. Dark waters splashed against the stern and Ecgtheow jerked his hand away. No telling what getting touched by that stuff would do to a man, and he didn't aim to be the one who found out.

Hervor rose, slow, and climbed over the side and onto

the bank. The others followed, leapt out one by one. When Ecgtheow had finally escaped the cursed craft, the ferryman pushed off with a long pole and set about drifting away, not a word more to her passengers. Which suited Ecgtheow well enough.

Sound of her voice set his teeth chattering.

As if they weren't enough already. A cold sweat ran down his neck and made the leathers beneath his mail sticky. He couldn't shake the shivers, though his guts felt like they were aflame. His shits had turned painful, runny things, as much blood as aught else. Whatever the hiidet had infected him with, it was eating him up and Wudga's salves only seemed to have delayed the inevitable.

Maybe Ecgtheow should've told the strange man, or the shaman, even. Except then they'd have asked him to wait behind, drink some foulness and sit and stew. If he was about to die—and he supposed he was—he'd just as soon go down with a blade in his hand instead of shitting himself to death.

Without a word, Hervor just started off, not even bothering for Pakkanen to lead the way. The shaman fell in beside her, looking about, before pointing off a slightly different direction. Hervor changed her stride, still saying naught.

The bitch had really caused all this with her murdering Orvar. If Ecgtheow died here, maybe she'd get away with it, too. Couldn't say he much liked that idea, but he liked the thought of Starkad wasting away even less.

So here he was.

And here, on the far bank, the land looked different. Darker even than the shadowy realm they'd just left. Like the rocks were a bit more jagged than he'd remembered, and black. Mighty obsidian daggers jutting up from the mountainside, ready to cleave through anyone who got too close.

Pretty much looking like a place straight out of a fever dream—or some skaldic rendition of the lands before Hel. All it needed was some snow and mist, and he'd expect to see the gates of the dark goddess's lands open up before them.

Ecgtheow grumbled under his breath as he walked. These days, he mused a great deal on what actions would make his ancestors proud. Even more so on making his son proud. In a situation like this, he found it hard to even know what that would be. If he didn't do aught about Hervor, he was almost as bad as her. If he did ... maybe he damned Starkad in the process. No good choices, those.

A rumbling shock shot through the ground and sent him tumbling down to one knee, along with most of the others. One of the obsidian shards split down the middle and a kobold leapt out. It was smaller than the ones he'd seen in Midgard, and more deformed. A hunchbacked frog-wolf thing with warty bulges covering nigh to every bit of its skin. A half dozen more strode out of other ruptured shards, even as Ecgtheow rose, pulling his sword.

The nearest kobold leapt in the air, croaking and slashing away with its claws. Ecgtheow dodged to the side, just out of its reach, and swept his broadsword. The blade bit into its gut and tore a gouge out that would've dropped a man. Instead, the beast let out another croak, this one almost a roar.

Another obsidian shard shattered. Pieces as big as Ecgtheow's hand flew at him. He flung up his arm reflexively. Jagged glass-like rocks sliced his flesh, tore open his brow. They screeched off his mail and drove him back. He looked down. A piece of obsidian was lodged into his fore-arm, right through the mail and between the bones.

Hardly even hurt.

Except now he was looking at it ... now it hurt. It *really* fucking hurt.

Ecgtheow looked up at the kobold he'd wounded. Creature stared at him with those hideous, bulging eyes, before leaping toward him. Ecgtheow jerked away, tried to bring his sword up, and found his arm was hardly working. No surprise, that.

Kustaa's axe caught the kobold in the back and drove it straight down into the ground before chopping it nigh in half. The pirate growled, trying to jerk his axe free with one hand, the other seeming half limp. Before he got it loose, another kobold leapt onto him and bowled him over.

Two-handing his sword to get a measure of control, Ecgtheow chopped down into the back of the new kobold's skull. Slime and brains gushed up out of the wound.

The pirate threw the creature off himself, regained his feet.

Hervor had already cut down two of the bastards from the look of it, blazing sword in hand. Wudga seemed to have felled the last of them. Least, Ecgtheow didn't see more, nor any glimmers to show they might be hiding. Hard to tell with these things, though.

Speaking of which, something about this had been bothering him. "How does Loviatar have kobolds in her service?" Ecgtheow asked. "I mean, aren't they vaettir?"

Wudga glanced at him for an instant before resuming scanning the surrounding area. "Sorcery. A sorcerer's primary power—besides knowledge—comes in the binding of vaettir. If she is strong enough, she may hold numerous vaettir to her will. Doing so comes at a horrible price, of course, as her humanity withers away. Sooner or later, those so bound break free and exact their revenge."

"Or maybe she has made a bargain with some greater power," Pakkanen added. "Such things are not for us to know. You would be happier not knowing the answers in any regard."

Tyrfing's blue flames seemed to grow ever more intense, and Ecgtheow suddenly realized Hervor was staring at him —staring hard.

Wudga slapped Hervor on the shoulder, though, and she grimaced, then blinked like she'd been half sleeping. Not a time to be getting groggy, far as Ecgtheow was concerned. They *all* needed to catch up on sleep. But not here. Not now.

The shieldmaiden sheathed the runeblade at last, eyes seeming half dead like she hadn't stopped acting for the ferryman. Ecgtheow couldn't say as he much enjoyed this place. Not in the least.

Pakkanen started off again, and they followed him for a short distance until the shaman held up a hand. "There is sorcery in the air. We draw nigh to our foe."

Worked for Ecgtheow. He was running out of time to make his glorious last stand and maybe earn the attention of a valkyrie to take him to Odin.

Before he could say aught about that, the sounds of battle reached them from beyond the next pass.

ho else would be fighting here? Another foe, most like, but still. If someone beset Loviatar's forces, the distraction might allow Hervor to move in for the kill. She'd deal with other foes later.

Keeping low, she crept up, around the edge of a boulder to peer down into a gulch ten feet below.

And she almost gasped.

In the midst of a trio of hiidet, a man spun, whipping a pair of swords around and fending off all three of them. Scraggly, looking burned and beaten and worse, still Starkad moved with uncanny speed, somehow able to keep at bay his vicious attackers.

How in Hel's bloody gates was Starkad here, in this realm? Was she dreaming? Was it another of the witch's illusions?

The man twisted, revealing a gaping, scorched hole where one of his eyes ought to have been.

Odin's blistered ...

The hiidet kept pushing in, and one scored a slash on Starkad's thigh that sent him staggering.

Not even he could hold the three of them off forever.

Well then, illusions be damned. Hervor rose, scurried to the edge of the gulch, and picked out a rock ledge halfway down. She jumped to this, then down again to bring her level with the melee. Then she pulled Tyrfing, roared, and raced in.

One of the hiidet spun on her, claws flashing. Tyrfing took its arm off at the wrist and ignited the wispy hairs above its lip. The creature staggered backward, clearly unaccustomed to a human with such ferocity. Hervor used its distraction to swing horizontally, a chop that cleanly severed its head from its body.

Not even a godsdamned hiisi kept fighting long without a head.

Starkad roared, now faced with only two foes, and managed to gouge the eye out of one with one blade while nicking the other in the knee. He shifted his momentum in a single fluid motion, jerking his first sword into the gut of the one he'd nicked while cutting out the throat of the other one.

Before Hervor could even bring Tyrfing back around, Starkad had whipped his blade in the opposite direction to smash in the impaled hiisi's skull.

Hervor let Tyrfing drop. "I don't know how you're here, but praise Odin that—"

Starkad roared, whipped the sword embedded in the hiisi free, and swung at her with the other.

Hervor stumbled backward, unable to bring Tyrfing up in time to parry. Starkad's blade sliced open a shallow cut across her abdomen. If she'd had her mail, it wouldn't have done much. As it was, it stung like Hel's own spit.

She jerked Tyrfing up and into position just in time to parry Starkad's other blade. "Starkad!"

He launched into relentless attacks, almost blindingly fast. In the space of a few heartbeats, he'd scored two more cuts on her—one to her calf, one to her arm. She twisted and parried, giving no thought to offense, just trying to keep those flashing blades off her.

"Starkad, it's me!" she shrieked.

Even the effort of speaking nigh cost her an ear as one of his swords drew a gouge along her cheekbone. So fast, the pain barely registered. Parry, dodge. "Starkad!"

She may have borne the flaming runeblade, but it did her no good if she couldn't manage to so much as swing it.

Clang! His sword rang out on hers. Hervor shrieked with fury, desperate to drive him back. He only moved faster.

"What happened to you?" Ecgtheow shouted from behind her.

Scuffling sounded, and then Wudga was there, parrying Starkad's swords on his own runeblade. Hervor could barely afford to glance at him. Fuck, but Starkad earned the name Eightarms. Hel, she might rather have fought *eight* different men instead of just four, if it meant not facing this onslaught.

"His travails have harrowed his mind," Pakkanen shouted from behind her. "Your friend cannot tell reality from illusion."

Wonderful. And what was she supposed to do about that?

"Eightarms!" Ecgtheow bellowed, now coming up as well, as did Kustaa, the two of them moving to flank Hervor's lover.

Kustaa swung that massive axe. Hervor's gut clenched as the blade descended on Starkad. No! Starkad twisted at the last instant, jerked the pommel of one sword back into Kustaa's face, shattering the pirate's nose and sending the man stumbling to the ground. Almost at the same instant, Starkad launched the blade forward at Wudga in a thrust that drove the man on the defensive.

His other sword parried Ecgtheow's counter, whipping up to slash the man in the face. A hair to the left or right and he'd have torn out the big man's eye. As it was, Ecgtheow blundered away, blood streaming from a cut that ran from his right cheek, across his nose, and over his left brow. A brutal scar, if he lived.

Hervor could've struck. She should strike. But one blow from Tyrfing ... one small cut ... and Starkad was a dead man. And all of this was for naught.

And that, she could not bear.

She backed away. He paused a brief moment, looked at her.

Hervor drove Tyrfing's point into the ground. As it left her grasp, the flames winked out. "Starkad ..."

With a growl, he whipped his swords around again, close to taking Wudga's head off. Wudga fell back, parried a second strike. He was losing ground fast.

Oh, Odin's giant balls. Hervor charged in, empty-handed, and dived for Starkad's abdomen, knowing she'd probably take a sword through her skull for her trouble. But he didn't turn quite fast enough, and she plowed into him, sent the both of them tumbling to the ground.

A fist cracked into her jaw and lights filled her vision. Buzzing drowned out sound. She was caught, heaved downward, thrown on the ground, a heavy weight atop her. A cold chill on her neck. The lights dimmed, just a bit, and Starkad was over her, blade pressed down against her throat. He had but to lean forward even a little ...

"Starkad," she mouthed.

His hand trembled and the blade bit through her flesh.

She felt the warm blood trickling down to the hollow of her throat.

"Please."

"You're not *real*."

"I am. I swear it."

The barest edge slipped from his grimace. A hint of doubt. He looked around, at Wudga, at Ecgtheow, at the other two he couldn't have known. Finally, he tossed his blade aside and grabbed his head, collapsing down atop her with enough force to knock her breath away.

Slowly, Hervor folded her arms around his back. "Starkad ..."

31

Starkad hardly seemed himself. Shouldn't have much surprised anyone, Ecgtheow supposed. Damn strange meeting someone you knew here, in this place. All he could figure was, the nightmare realm Starkad inhabited, and this Tuonela were either the same, or close enough they touched one another and the man had passed between the two.

Either way, though, the man walked like he was in a daze, stuck close to Hervor.

Which, unfortunately, made it difficult to catch him aside and let him know about the shieldmaiden's part in this all. There she was with him, so close as to erase any doubt left that the two of them were fucking fair regular, and her playing him for a fool. Hervor had murdered Starkad's own friend and now shared his bed.

A cold trick, that, and it didn't sit well with Ecgtheow. Starkad had a right to know the truth, but it seemed best to tell him in private, without the shieldmaiden there to try and spin it round. She was a practiced liar, after all. Last thing anyone needed was her getting the chance to weave another web around them all.

Hel, who knew what she'd been whispering in his ear this past hour? Naught good, Ecgtheow supposed. He frowned, shaking his head at the pair of them.

"Jealous?" Kustaa asked, words a muffled whine through his broken nose.

Ecgtheow cast him a half-hearted frown. "Finally chose to speak, and *that's* what you've got to say now? That I'm jealous of Starkad?"

Kustaa grunted. "Me. Jealous."

Huh? Oh. "Count yourself lucky, my friend. The shield-maiden is more trouble than she's worth."

Kustaa just grunted again.

"Here," Wudga whispered from the head of the group. He had ducked down atop a ridge overlooking a valley. Mountains were strange in this land—no snow. Just rock and shadows.

Hervor and Starkad went crawling up beside Wudga, so Ecgtheow supposed he'd best have a look himself. Climbing up there winded him, though, and he was huffing by the time he reached the top. By then, the others had already started to skirt down the other side, swift but stealthy.

And there she was hiding in the valley, the witch-queen herself. Except here, her beauty had withered and left a hag in its place, one with bulging growths bubbling out of her exposed shoulders. Her neck bore slits like gills, spewing out some no-doubt toxic gas. The worst of it though—her missing eyes were whole here, globes of green luminescent jelly.

A trio of kobolds circled her, croaking about whatever the witch had told them. If there was only the three of them, Ecgtheow supposed that meant she was running low on minions just about now. A good sign, that, since he figured he was running low on time himself.

Even standing enough to crest the rise hurt, sent his guts churning.

Best get this over with. He scrambled down after the others and Pakkanen glanced back at him, face stern. Maybe the shaman had some idea what was eating away at Ecgtheow. Funny, he'd have expected the rot in his body to hold no sway over his soul wandering around this place. Suppose the two must be connected after all. Either way, Pakkanen nodded at him, then turned back to the task at hand.

Eightarms and Hervor were just at the bottom of the valley when the kobolds set to their rapid croaking, scrambling off to meet them. The witch curled her lip at Hervor, then fled into a cave in the rocks.

With luck, there wouldn't be another way out of that hole. Sadly, Ecgtheow hadn't had overmuch luck on his side of late.

The kobolds leapt from one obsidian shard to the next, crawling over them like lizards and hopping like frogs. They didn't vanish from sight though. Did that mean that power only worked in the real world? If so, he'd have to thank Odin for even a small boon.

Ecgtheow pulled his sword and trotted forward, each step painful, struggling not to topple over as he ran down the slope.

One of the kobolds made the mistake of leaping at Starkad. Two blades diced the beast into pieces before it even landed. The other leapt away from Hervor's flaming runeblade only to find itself impaled on Wudga's cursed sword. Pair of vicious bastards, them, but Ecgtheow supposed he was lucky they were along. At least for now.

Hervor cut down the last of the kobolds, turned, and

raced straight into the cave. Not one for planning overmuch, then.

Ecgtheow grunted, sucked down a painful breath, and sprinted for the opening, his left leg trying to give out with each step.

He reached the cave last, a few steps behind Pakkanen. The shaman had pulled up short inside. Everyone had, all transfixed by the swaying head of a serpent at least a hundred feet long.

In the swamp, he'd not gotten too close a look at Ajatar. Everything had happened so fast, and it was so damned dark ... Here, though, the dragon was revealed in all its hideous glory. Wing-like protrusions jutted from the back of its head, toxins spewing out behind them. Venom dripped from curving fangs as big as Ecgtheow was. Awkward arms seeming small next to its bulk, but still tipped with massive claws.

The abomination's coils encircled Loviatar, made it impossible to charge the witch without running right under the serpent's mouth. Ecgtheow's stomach lurched, clenching and unclenching. His fingers had gone so limp, so clammy, he was surprised the sword hadn't fallen from his grasp.

Fucking ... huge.

They'd barely escaped it last time ... when they had somewhere to run.

Now ...

Hel.

"It passes between realms ..." Pakkanen said, seeming like he was half talking to himself.

Ecgtheow shook himself. He wanted a glorious death ... "Time to earn your keep, shaman." He hefted his sword back up. Naught for it, really. If he ran, the serpent would catch him and kill him anyway. If he somehow escaped, he'd probably be dead of the sickness not long after. Just one way this could go.

"You killed a dragon before," Hervor said, presumably to Starkad.

"Smaller."

The dragon roared, the sound echoing through the cavern, setting the ground and walls to trembling.

Yeah, fuck it all. Ecgtheow bellowed a war cry and raced straight for that gaping maw.

The serpent surged forward and its coils battered into Ecgtheow and Pakkanen both, sending them tumbling through the air and slamming down hard on the rock floor. Obsidian stalactites crashed down from above, shattering, exploding into shards. Ecgtheow knew he was screaming, hands over his head, but couldn't quite stop.

The moment the crashing stopped, he struggled to his feet.

Loviatar had closed the distance to them and caught Pakkanen by the throat, hefting him up until his toes barely brushed the ground. "Little shaman ... thinks to match with *me*?" She opened her mouth wide, exposing a black void. Then she drew Pakkanen's face up close and hissed, spraying what looked like ash over the shaman's face.

The witch dropped him as Ecgtheow advanced, and the shaman fell to his knees, coughing, clutching his throat. His skin turned purple, and he heaved like he meant to retch, except only ashes came out. Ashes—and a stream of black blood dribbling over his lips. Then seeping from his nose. Then his ears. Pakkanen was screaming.

Ecgtheow faltered, unable to make himself move forward toward the wickedly grinning witch.

Pustules rose up all over Pakkanen's face and arms. Then they burst, spewing blood and pus out in geysers. A man shouldn't be able to scream like that. Shouldn't be able to live through aught which would draw out such a sound. Pakkanen rocked back and forth, wailed. Then his eyes exploded like the pustules had, spraying out more gore. And the shaman pitched face-first into the ground.

An enormous crash sounded behind Ecgtheow. A roar. A hiss. He'd forgotten about the fucking dragon. And still, he could not look away from the witch, as she strode toward him. He had his broadsword up, one hand steadying the other, and still they were trembling.

Her flesh was rotting, something like maggots wriggling around beneath her skin.

Vulgar, blasphemous nightmare what shouldn't have existed.

Ecgtheow was breathing too fast. He couldn't control his heartbeat.

A battle cry, behind him, and Kustaa charged past, swinging his axe in wide arcs, vicious. Wild, without proper control from one hand. But fearless. The way Ecgtheow had been … a lifetime ago. Now he felt half a craven, beaten down by the unending horrors of the Otherworlds.

Die bravely and see the valkyries.

Die bravely.

When all he wanted to see was his wife and child.

Loviatar caught Kustaa's axe by its haft. The wood rotted beneath her grasp, turning black and then crumbling, leaving the axe-head to tumble down and clatter onto the stone.

Die … bravely.

Ecgtheow roared his own battle cry and charged the witch.

32

The dragon recoiled from Tyrfing's flame as Hervor whipped the runeblade around again. Her arms felt afire themselves, aching, and she knew each swing grew slower than the last. She could not keep this up for long.

Starkad had scored several small gashes on the dragon's face, once each time it tried to lunge for him. He was brave and fast—faster than any man she'd ever seen—but they were still only human.

The dragon slammed its coils into the cavern wall again, sending another shower of obsidian shards raining down from above. Hervor dove to the side, hands over her head, screaming.

Black rocks clattered harmlessly off the dragon's scaled hide, but one slammed into the ground a hairsbreadth from where Starkad stood, cracked open the stone, and stood there, embedded. Hervor's lover just dodged around it, swept his own sword around, and cleaved into the dragon's scales.

Or tried.

His blades clattered off the dragon's hide as ineffective as the rocks had been.

Odin, give them strength.

From the far side, Wudga charged in, spun, and whipped Mimung down. His runeblade sheared through dragon scale almost as easily as it carved through mortal armor. The creature's blood shot out in a geyser, hissing like acid and sending Wudga scrambling away to avoid getting scorched.

Ajatar bellowed and spun on Wudga in fury.

Hervor used the opportunity to cleave into its length with Tyrfing. Already prepared, she dove under the spray of acid blood, twisted around, and jerked the flaming sword up once more.

The creature shrieked, but it was like trying to kill a mammoth with a thousand cuts from a dagger. Even if it finally worked, everyone involved would be squashed in the process.

Hervor twisted around to see the dragon had now turned its gaze on her. She froze for a split second, then dove to the side, behind a fallen obsidian shard.

A heartbeat later, the dragon's maw crashed into the spot she'd stood, its fangs gouging even the stone floor, a chunk of which it spit out at Wudga. The man threw himself prone to avoid it.

Another war cry. Somehow, Starkad had gotten atop the linnorm's body and was running up its length, toward its head. His steps uneven, pain obvious in his visage.

Hervor gaped. Mist-madness at its finest. He was *running* on a dragon. He was ...

She shook her head, not quite able to believe he'd even try that.

Nor did the dragon itself seem to believe it. It threw its

head violently against the wall. Rather than be crushed, Starkad jumped, swords pointed down, and let his momentum add weight to his strikes. One of the blades actually managed to embed itself between two scales. As Starkad fell, the scale peeled back and popped clean off, spraying acid and some foul gas in the process.

Starkad landed and sprang up almost in one move, driving his other sword through the now exposed flesh. It sunk up to the hilt, and the dragon convulsed, reared back, and roared.

Shit. It was going to fucking kill him.

Hervor charged forward, slashing as she ran, drawing numerous cuts along Ajatar's scales. Acid droplets sprayed over her, scorching her skin. She grit her teeth against the pain and kept hacking away, desperate to keep it from focusing on Starkad.

Wudga must have sensed her plan, because she heard him screaming, hewing away at the dragon's tail. She spared him a glance. The serpent lunged forward. Its coils slapped into Wudga as it moved. Volund's son flew backward and hurtled into the cavern wall, then fell limp and lay still.

In the chaos and noise of the fight, Hervor had no idea if he yet drew breath. Nor could she spare even a moment to check in on the man.

Starkad had lost one of his swords—damn, it was still stuck in the dragon—and was now desperately fending off the beast's maw with the other. His face had turned green as the dragon's breath fell over him. Odin alone knew what poisons where in that gas.

If she ever needed Tyrfing, now was the time. If the runeblades had ever been intended for a noble purpose, let Tyrfing now kill this creature. Hervor shrieked and thrust Tyrfing deep into dragon flesh. Rather than jerk it free, she grabbed it with both hands and pulled it straight across, running forward as she did so.

Fresh acid sprayed over her hands, scorched them, and she shrieked in agony but refused to let go of the sword. Blue flames erupted beneath the dragon's scales. Its flesh split apart at the seams, drawing a gaping hole that just kept growing.

Acid and blood and gore stung her eyes, blinded her. She kept pulling. Her arms were ready to fall off. Just a little more ... She jerked the runeblade along, shredding the dragon like a sausage, screaming in fury and agony all the while.

The runeblade scraped bone. Cut through it and kept going. The dragon's flailing caught her, sent her tumbling along the ground. Tyrfing slipped from her grasp and went out.

Her head slammed against the rock and white light filled her vision. Ears ringing ... Maybe dying ...

Roaring echoed through the cavern.

Hervor blinked, tried to focus.

"My arm!"

She turned. Loviatar had caught Kustaa's forearm. Where she'd grabbed him, his flesh had turned rotten, blackening as it bubbled and peeled. A creeping pestilence spread up his arm as the witch released him. Edging closer and closer to his elbow.

Kustaa was screaming, eyes wide in horror at his decaying body.

Ecgtheow bellowed and brought his broadsword down, severing Kustaa's arm at the elbow. The dismembered limb fell, hit the ground. Continued to blacken and rot with an acrid stench. Flesh ate away revealing bone beneath, and even that began to crack.

Kustaa had fallen to his knees, cradling his arm, while Ecgtheow spun after Loviatar. Except the witch was missing.

Hervor pushed herself up, crawling to where Tyrfing lay fallen.

Turned over.

Starkad shrieked as he drove a blade through Ajatar's eye. Acid exploded over him and he fell, screaming, rolling on the ground. The dragon reared back, bucked wildly, slamming against the cavern walls.

Twice, and then it collapsed down to the floor. It heaved and hissed. Some foulness Hervor couldn't identify dribbled out of Ajatar's mouth.

Starkad thrashed, screaming. And then he seemed to melt through the floor.

Hervor scrambled over to where he'd just lain, fell to her hands, and beat the empty floor. It was acid-scorched, but no sign remained of her lover.

She pounded the rock once more but got no answer.

WHILE ECGTHEOW WAS TYING off Kustaa's wound, Wudga came limping around the dead linnorm's coils, holding his ribs and wheezing with each breath he took. No disguising the pain in his eyes. How many ribs had the dragon broken? A lot, more like than not, and still Hervor counted him lucky to be walking at all. She knew that pain all too well.

"He was right here," she mumbled under her breath.

Wudga groaned, shook his head. "With Pakkanen dead ... our only way back to the realm of the living now lies through Loviatar's own power. We ... need ... need to be there if she opens that way. If we ... miss ..."

Oh, Odin's balls. If they missed it, they'd be trapped here

forever. Or until they died, which was not like to be long at this rate.

"All right!" she snapped. "We have to move, now!" The witch must've had another exit from this place. Hervor glanced back at the entrance. Unless she could turn invisible like the damn hiidet. "Wudga. Can you find her trail?"

"I'm not a shaman." He grunted in discomfort. "I don't … there's another tunnel out of this chamber, beyond the linnorm's coils."

No guarantee Loviatar had gone that route, but they had to try. "Make for it." And pray to Odin that the witch-queen had fled in that direction.

Ecgtheow helped Kustaa up, but the pirate shrugged him off and hefted a torch with his remaining hand. Hervor didn't envy him trying to fight with his off-hand—especially if that was the broken arm. It had taken Hervor a lot of moons training left-handed with Starkad to come anywhere nigh to the skill she'd had with her right. Still probably wasn't there yet—and never would be. But those first moons, those were the worst.

The four of them edged around the dragon corpse and then made their way into the tunnel Wudga indicated. Hervor led the way, using Tyrfing's flames as a torch as she pushed on.

The passage sloped downward for a hundred feet or so before leveling out. The tunnel looked more like a burrow. Maybe Ajatar had dug this out herself. Either way, it soon opened out into a small cavern honeycombed by other tunnels.

The witch stood at the mouth of one, speaking to more hiidet. A half dozen of those trollfuckers. Loviatar and her minions all paused as Hervor entered the cavern. All looked to her, to Tyrfing flaming in her hand. Hervor glared at the queen of Loude, panting through her clenched teeth. This time, the queen would die.

Bellowing, Hervor charged straight in at the hiidet. She'd expected them to vanish, but instead they dove *into* the rocks, disappearing underground. She faltered a step, then hesitated. The stone just before her rose like a bubble out of water. Then one of the creatures burst forth from it, croaking and slashing.

Hervor swept Tyrfing down on its head, splattering the creature. More popped up around her.

Damn it. Godsdamned diminutive globs of troll shit! She roared, whipping Tyrfing around. "Wudga! Go after Loviatar."

The man raced past her, dodging around another breaking stone bubble, and took off toward the witch—who began to run down the tunnel. Wudga's uneven gait revealed his pain, but he was moving. And he was resistant to her Art, it seemed—maybe the best suited to kill Loviatar.

"You two, help me take out these hiidet!"

Ecgtheow bellowed in assent and laid into the nearest one. Kustaa, though, just kept running right after Wudga and Loviatar.

Hervor gaped at him, shook her head. Bastard wanted revenge on the bitch who took his arm. She couldn't blame him, but his timing might cost them all.

Shrieking, Hervor barely dodged one of a hiisi's rending claws. Another tore into her unprotected side.

Tyrfing severed the hand that had struck her. Sweat and blood and gore blinded her, and she spun, using the flames to hold the monsters at bay as much as to strike at them. Ecgtheow had felled one and now brought his blade down in a vicious overhead chop on the fallen hiisi.

Hervor turned, cut through the last one she could see,

though more bubbles seemed to flow beneath the ground. "We have to get after the witch."

Ecgtheow grunted, nodded, and took off in that direction, half running, half limping. The big man had been through a lot. A lot of it with her. And now he was going to fuck things up with Starkad.

Which she couldn't allow.

She trotted after him, then swiped Tyrfing across his hamstring as she passed. The blade bit through flesh with ease and ignited his trousers. Ecgtheow fell, screaming in agony and rolling on the ground.

Hervor couldn't bring herself to even look back as she ran on. Killing Loviatar and saving Starkad were what mattered. Ecgtheow ... one more murder. One more betrayal ...

Because what choice did he leave her?

Bastard.

She raced down the tunnel, panting with the effort. The route opened into another small cavern, this one deep below, and reachable by a path that wrapped around the outskirts. At the base of it, maybe forty feet down, a chunk of white root had burst through the stone floor.

Even as Hervor entered, Loviatar had her hand against the root. Was making it morph.

Odin's flaming balls!

Wudga charged after her, Kustaa a half step behind and roaring like a madman.

She'd never make it. She'd be trapped here just like Ecgtheow. Fuck that. She jumped from the path onto where it wrapped around, fell almost twenty feet, and landed in a roll. The impact sent a jolt through her, and she almost tumbled down off the side the rest of the way.

"Trollfuckers," she grunted, then threw herself down again, and hit the ground hard.

It stole her breath and left the room spinning, but she scrambled to her feet and dashed.

Kustaa had passed through the opening. Already, the root wall was closing.

Heaving. Gasping in pain and exhaustion. And utter fucking desperation. She flung herself forward, and the root snapped back into place behind her. She tumbled to the ground, rolled and couldn't rise. Her arms wouldn't answer.

She sucked in a painful breath. Looked up. She was laying on the floor in the same room they'd begun the vision quest in. No sign of Höfund. Ecgtheow's body was still there, slumped over in sleep.

Loviatar stood nearby, turning around as if searching in vain for something. Her guise had switched back to the beautiful, eyeless maiden. Save for black hands outstretched, grasping, reaching for them.

Kustaa roared and launched himself at her, waving his torch—the only light source in this place. Loviatar jerked around suddenly, ducked a blow she clearly couldn't have seen, and caught him on the back of the neck with a black hand. His legs gave out beneath him, and his skin turned ashen. A moment later, it began to rupture, spewing blood and black filth in all directions. The pirate spasmed, screaming in pain Hervor didn't even want to consider.

She slowly stood. Started to reach for Tyrfing on the ground. Loviatar dropped Kustaa and looked around. Listening.

The only sound came from the faint crackle of Kustaa's fallen torch.

If Hervor picked up the runeblade, the witch might hear it.

Where was Wudga?

There. Lying on the floor, not far from where the root had been. Must've gotten hurt on the way through. Running with multiple broken ribs—probably not healthy.

Loviatar stalked around the room, fingers clenching and unclenching. Eager to catch Hervor, no doubt. "I know you're here."

Hervor willed her breath to slow, held it, as the blind witch passed within a foot of her. She dared not move a muscle. Any sound and Loviatar would catch her out.

Loviatar turned again, waving that black hand out in front of herself. Hervor leaned backward, away from it as those wretched fingers passed dangerously close to her nose.

The witch moved on, toward Wudga's prone form. Closed in on him. "Afraid, little girl?" At this point, Hervor worried her pounding heart would give her away. "I suppose I'll settle for this one, then. For now."

Hervor grimaced. Wudga. Damn it. Her hand closed around the hilt of her dagger. If the witch heard her advance ... One touch and she was dead. In a rather horrific manner, from the look of it.

So she had to close in, silent as death. Had to kill her with one blow of the dagger and make sure Loviatar couldn't touch her in the process. Sounded all but impossible.

Starkad was counting on her.

So.

So fear and the witch could both go fuck a troll.

Hervor flung the dagger. It wasn't weighted for throwing, of course. Hardly mattered since she only aimed at the far wall.

Loviatar spun at the sound of it clattering. Hervor used

the noise to snatch up Tyrfing, then immediately thrust the runeblade forward. The witch spun, but too late. The runeblade slipped through her side, hit the spine, then punched out the other way. Hervor jerked the blade back immediately, falling over herself to get out of reach of the suddenly grasping black hands.

The witch flailed around limply, her death grasp passing nigh to Hervor's knees, even as her torso seemed ready to pitch over to one side or another.

On her arse, Hervor scrambled backward, knowing Tyrfing scraped over stone and she made an awful racket, but unable to do aught about it.

Loviatar hissed like a fucking snake, spun around, and retched up a curtain of black blood that fell just short of where Hervor lay. The witch shambled forward, reaching for her.

Screaming, Hervor rolled to the side, swiping with the runeblade. It cleanly severed Loviatar's leg at the knee, and the witch toppled over and fell face-first into the stone floor.

Hervor shrieked, rose up, and cleaved the witch's skull in two. Then she hacked into the corpse a half dozen more times.

HERVOR LIMPED BACK DOWN the walkway around the World Pillar, Wudga leaning on her shoulder. The dark-haired man had drifted in and out of lucidity all the way, but they were almost there. Loviatar's minions were, thankfully, nowhere to be seen.

In the distance, she caught sight of Höfund, limping back toward them. Must've chased off some more warriors

—though it meant leaving their bodies defenseless. Hervor frowned at that.

"I ... uh ... what happened to Ecgtheow?" Wudga said.

Hervor flinched, keeping her eyes on the pillar up ahead. She'd done what she had to do. The man had brought it on himself. "He fell to the hiidet."

"Mmm."

Shit. What did that mean? Did Wudga now doubt her as well? It would be more than unfortunate if he too failed to return from Pohjola. With Odin's blessing, maybe it wouldn't come to that. She actually rather liked him, truth be told.

Together, they returned to the base of the pillar. Väinämöinen had claimed he'd know when Loviatar fell. And the witch was dead.

Tyrfing had seen to that.

Repeatedly.

Beneath the walkway, a figure knelt, a man of ashen skin and jet-black hair. The man had pounded a spike into the root and was collecting sap draining from it in a skin. And she knew him.

"Volund."

The svartalf spared her the merest glance, a hint of a wry grin upon his face, then resumed his work.

Hervor turned to Wudga at her side. He didn't seem surprised to see his father.

Not surprised, because they'd been working together all along ...

She shoved Wudga off her shoulder and he stumbled a few steps but managed to keep his feet. "You bastard."

Wudga quirked a smile. "I never denied my parentage."

She swiveled her gaze back and forth from father to son.

"You planned this? You chose this mission ... Because you're working with the wizard, aren't you?"

Now Volund did fix her with his own dark gaze and, despite herself, Hervor backed away a step. "Tell me, shield-maiden, have you kin left to you? And, with precious few remaining, would you not go to extraordinary lengths to aid those yet by your side?"

"You are kin to Väinämöinen ... both of you." Odin's balls. She had not seen this coming. "Men from Kvenland ..." She backed away another step. "You had me kill the witch so you could access the World Pillar." She licked her parched lips. All of it snapping into place. "The World Pillar is a root of the World Tree ... but you cannot access the tree itself. The Aesir have claimed it."

Volund quirked his knowing grin and said naught more. And Wudga, that bastard, didn't even meet her gaze, just limped over to where his father worked.

Hervor had the sickening sensation of being a pawn in a game so large she couldn't even see the board. Gods and alfar and sorcerers moved the lives of men about, caring naught for what befell those pieces ... "Starkad ... Did you orchestrate his affliction?"

Volund chuckled. "If you seek someone to blame for your lover's condition, you have need not look far, shield-maiden. Sometimes, one needs but take advantage of circumstances already in existence."

Hervor spit. Her hand clinched around Tyrfing's hilt over her shoulder. Maybe he was a svartalf. An immortal. A vaettr. But then again, she'd fought immortals before. "Did Väinämöinen ever intend to aid Starkad?"

Again, that dark, infuriating chuckle. Volund bent, snatched up the skin filled with sap, and rose. And then, before her eyes, his form shifted, shrunk. In the space of a few heartbeats, he'd become a raven. With a startling caw, he took flight and disappeared into the night sky.

Leaving her and Wudga alone. She glanced to where Höfund was still limping closer, though he was yet far off. "I ought to kill you."

Wudga shook his head. "You could try. And yet … your quest succeeded. Would it have, had not I been there? As my father has said, are you not largely to blame for this yourself?"

He *did* know. Maybe he'd always known. Told by his father, perhaps. Whispers from the shadows.

And if she drew Tyrfing, there would be no turning back.

"Consider, Hervor. Had Väinämöinen not come to you, where would Starkad be now?"

"He was *your* friend, too."

Wudga nodded. "Then we are both lucky the quest was accomplished."

At the cost of a lot of lives.

Finally, Hervor released Tyrfing's hilt. Maybe there had been enough blood for one day.

With a shake of her head, she turned and started for Höfund. The two of them would have a long, painful journey out of Pohjola.

When she glanced back, Wudga was gone.

33

*D*eath, when it comes with a certainty, hardly felt a burden anymore. Maybe the burden, the fear, came from knowing you might die. Staring right in its face without the merest chance of survival, that didn't leave much room for fear, Ecgtheow supposed.

What was the point of fearing something that could only go one way?

Urd had come for him at last.

His broadsword dragged behind him, scraping over the obsidian stones all around.

The wound in his leg gave him a mighty limp, had to be said, and burned like Hel's spit. Not just the fires, either, he supposed. Tyrfing had a poison to it, already scorching through his veins.

Poison wouldn't kill him, though.

The horde of kobolds, croaking and hopping about the twisted landscape before him—they'd be the ones to do it. At least two dozen of the little trollfuckers.

Better than dying of poison, he supposed.

He continued on toward the pack of hideous creatures,

spitting out a glob of blood and mucus and Hel knew what else. And those kobolds, they didn't bother closing in. Not when he was coming right to them. They knew it, sure as he did. There just wasn't a damn place left to go here.

All the doors were closed.

A man came here, after he died, assuming you believed shamans like Pakkanen. So what happened to a man who died and was already in this place? That thought gave him pause. And maybe a hint of the fear coming back, truth be told.

What happened to your soul if you died already in the land of the dead? Would valkyries come for him at all?

A bit of uncertainty, and back came the burden, the fear taunting him.

Suppose he would find out the answer soon though.

He drew up his sword before him and let out the best growl he could manage.

Almost as one, the kobolds erupted in a wave of croaking, slobbering chaos headed for him.

All that remained now was to give a death his ancestors could be proud of. To make a stand that would honor Ylva. To fight one last time, so little Beowulf could think of his father's name with pride.

One final battle.

Ecgtheow roared defiance at those little fuckers.

34

The darkness shifted around Starkad, writhing in waves and melding with the twisted landscape of jagged obsidian peaks. He couldn't remember how he'd gotten here. He'd been with Hervor not too long ago and then ... Just lost in the dark. Wandering through a miasma of shadows and chaos, ever seeking any sign of light.

A faint glow in the sky with no apparent source kept him out of total blackness, true, but he could make out so little in the distance, it made it hard to choose a destination. Hard to even be certain he had not wandered in circles for the past hour.

"Did you think I would let you go?" The feminine voice emerged from the darkness behind him.

Starkad spun and backed away. It took a moment to focus on the form lounging upon an obsidian shelf level with his head. She laid back, arms and legs splayed, completely naked. It was Ogn, but not as she had been in life, nor even as she'd seemed when he saw her in Alfheim.

She still had the elongated, purple tongue, flicking between a maw of irregular fangs. But now, a half dozen black spiraling horns jutted from her skull, parting her blonde hair. Her fingers ended in claws. Tattered, bat-like wings flopped lazily against the rock, jutting from her back. Darkness swirled in her eyes. A serpentine tail twitched by her side. Black fluid oozed from her trench as she rubbed at it with a single finger.

"It ought to have broken you," she purred. "Left you so hollow that I might have sucked you dry." She pursed her lips and ran her tongue over them, somehow leaving him both hard and nauseated all at once. "But I want more than your seed, my darling. I want all that you are or ever could have been." She chuckled, then moaned, as if all this excited her, as if actually pleasuring herself. "Oh ... Dear sweet Starkad. You ought to have broken in half and been left a weeping wreck of what you once were."

Here she was. Afzal had warned him he must confront her if he was to win his way free. Every instinct begged him to turn away from the horror and temptation she represented. To do so, or else to rush into it her, bury himself in her so deep he'd never have to come out again. Fighting both urges, he clenched his jaw and scowled. Shook his head. "Maybe I'm stronger than you thought."

She snorted. "That fool wizard interfered." She frowned and gnawed on her lower lip with those hideous fangs. "Thought to help you with his pathetic little bird. Without it, the worlds of the Spirit Realm would have left you a shriveled, shrieking mess long before you passed through them all."

"But I survived. It must vex you ..."

Now she grinned, and leapt off the rock, tail twitching as she stalked closer. Ogn drew a clawed hand along the line of his collarbone as she stalked around him, purring. "Do you think you have seen the extent of the horrors the Otherworlds hold for the souls of men? Do you think the Spirit Realm is the farthest, darkest realm to which I might take you?" She cackled. "Does it give you courage to believe the worst is behind you?" She backed away, shaking her head and snickering. "When you have not yet witnessed the extent of *these* realms, what hope for you might lay in the realms beyond ..."

Beyond the Spirit Realm? As in, further than the worlds of the vaettir. The thought had never occurred to him. Was it an idle threat? Did aught even exist beyond the extreme worlds he'd already visited? Starkad shook his head, unwilling to let her send him back on the defensive. "I loved you, Ogn."

"You killed me."

Had he? He'd killed her lover, the father of her child, though at the time, he hadn't known Hergrimr was either of those things. "I tried to save you. I made a mistake, maybe. Maybe many. But you took your own godsdamned life. I didn't force you to that. I came intending to marry you, and then, finding you missing, to save you from your abductor."

"I didn't need saving!" she screeched. A beat of her wings carried her aloft, several feet away from him. "I didn't ask you to come there!"

He spread his hands and shook his head. "You never stopped haunting me. For years, you were the shadow in my dreams, my guilt. I thought it guilt ... but was that really you? Have you in truth become a mara? I think you have."

"I am what you made me."

Starkad grimaced. "I had a hand in it. But you ... you have become what your rage made you. What your own suicide made you. Whatever nightmare you fell into, whatever it shaped you into, you jumped in of your own volition."

She lunged forward with uncanny speed, her claws embedding in his shoulders. She bore him down to the ground and slammed him hard upon the rocks. "You loved me? You *loved* me? Love me *now*!" With one hand she pinned both of his up behind him. With the other she grabbed his trousers. Her claws shredded the laces and she jerked them open. "I'm going to suck your life out through your cock, you sniveling wretch!"

Her bulbous tongue lathered over him, forcing an undesired response from his body. Starkad jerked his knee up and caught her under the jaw. The impact drove her teeth into her tongue and she jerked away, releasing his hands and grabbing her tongue with one of her own. She spat out a glob of dark blood and hissed at him even as he rose.

"I'm going to enjoy forcing you to pleasure me. To tongue me for days on end. When you are dying of thirst, the only liquid to pass your lips will be—" Ogn stumbled, clutched both hands to her head and shrieked, doubling over in pain.

The sound of her cry rent through Starkad's mind like a hot iron and sent him reeling too.

Strange, alien words like those of vaettir vaguely reverberated off the obsidian walls. He dropped to his knees. The world grew hazy, fading in and out of focus.

"No!" Ogn bellowed. "No! Silence, song-crafter! I'll bite your tongue clean off!"

Starkad jolted to realize he was saying the same words as Ogn. That her voice was coming from his throat. "I'll drag your soul screaming into the abyss! The horrors this one faced will seem but pale amusements compared to what I'll—"

Another of her shrieks stole her words and stopped Starkad's as well.

A flame rose inside him, a heat like something was ripping him in half. Darkness closed all around him.

He slammed head-first into the ground. His body convulsed, thrashed, banging his skull against the rocks over and over.

Until everything went black.

§

STARKAD GROANED. Blinked. A haze of flickering firelight stung his eyes. Both his eyes. He had two, although he could see naught from one, and the other seemed cloudy as well. He lay in a bed, in a dark room.

The only sound came from the crackle of a brazier and the faint panting of another man, slumped upon the floor. Starkad sat, then pitched straight out of the bed finding he had not the least bit of strength left in him.

His legs felt pulverized. His ribs battered. His skin felt aflame. His stomach rumbled as if he had not eaten in a moon or more.

And his head felt as though a troll had jumped up and down on it.

Groaning, he managed to look up at the other man. That was ... the singer from Kvenland. Blond hair, streaked with gray. Simple clothes.

The singer ... the wizard.

"What happened?" Starkad's throat was raw, cracked.

The other man rubbed his face. Now that Starkad looked closer, a sheen of sweat covered the Kvenlander's brow. "I exorcised the mara with a song."

"Exorcised ... You cast her out. She's ... she's still out there."

The Kvenlander chuckled lightly. "If beings from beyond

our realm can be destroyed, such matters lie far beyond human Art. But those cast out through exorcism or the destruction of their hosts, they pay a price for it. It takes them time to regain their strength, or so some believe. Either way, she is out of you."

Maybe. But Ogn hated Starkad, blamed him for all that had befallen her, and not entirely without cause.

"Yes," the Kvenlander said, as if reading his face. "They are eternal, so far as I know."

"She'll come after me again. If not in life, then …"

The man frowned in apparent sympathy.

Starkad shook himself. Whatever had happened, it was past. "Hervor. Where is she?"

"Off in Kvenland. She fought for you and won. I imagine now she already makes her way back, seeking you."

Starkad struggled to push himself up, but only managed his knees. "I have to go there, have to meet her."

The other man shook his head. "You have not the strength to step outside for a piss. You will be long in recovering from such an ordeal, I think. And some of what you lost will not return."

Starkad put a hand to his eye, waved it front of his face, then blanched at being unable to see it. "You're a sorcerer."

"If you prefer the term. Men call workers of the Art by so many titles, and all apply, or none, perhaps. I am a singer of songs."

Starkad swallowed, shook himself.

Ogn had taken a great deal from him, it seemed. Some of it, he couldn't quite remember. Much of what he did recall, he wished he didn't. A haze had settled on his memories, and not just those from the nightmare worlds. His past, his childhood, he could feel things were missing now. Gone from him, like faded dreams, leaving only the impressions of events that might once have seemed clear.

Such was the price of his survival.

She had taken from him.

But maybe she had given something to him as well.

In the end, Hervor had come for him. Crossed this world and the Otherworlds to find him. And maybe she had become all he'd once dreamed Ogn might be.

Something worth living for.

EPILOGUE

The song came to him, tickled his wandering and restless mind, and pulled him from dreams he'd have chosen not to leave behind. The song, peaceful and beautiful, stole Odin's reprieve from him.

Waters poured away from him in great showers as the mud shoved him up, rejecting his presence within the lake. It parted around him, guiding him back to the shore like a mighty hand, and left him to retch forth the fluid choking his lungs.

Odin convulsed. Shivered. Looked up at Väinämöinen as the wizard's song finally ended. And beauty and peace shattered around Odin as silence settled in.

He coughed up more water, then turned to glare up at the song-crafter through his drenched gray hair.

"A move is made, and the turn is passed, so chance must be given once again."

Odin panted, half-frozen. So, Väinämöinen had accomplished whatever aim he'd intended—whatever end he'd kept Odin imprisoned for. And now he was releasing Odin, clearly not intending to murder him. Probably a mistake.

Odin surged strength into his limbs from the power the apple had given him. He launched himself upward faster than most men could have hoped to have reacted. One hand he clutched around Väinämöinen's throat, the other he slapped over the song-crafter's mouth. Growling, Odin hefted the man off the ground and into the air and charged away from the lake like that. He carried the Kvenlander several steps until he could slam him against a tree.

The song-crafter's eyes glazed over and it took a moment before the man even seemed to come around again. When he did, when he focused on Odin, his visage revealed a satisfying hint of fear.

"Your first mistake," Odin said, then paused to catch his breath. "Your first mistake was using your Art against *me*. The second mistake was not killing me when you had the chance." Odin squeezed a little harder. Väinämöinen had wrapped his hands around Odin's wrist, tugging on it. He might as well have been trying to bend iron with his bare hands. "I wonder, *friend*. Do you think I am like to make that same mistake? To let you live after so accosting me? Or perhaps I ought to simply tear your tongue from your mouth and leave you forever mourning the loss."

Väinämöinen raised his hands in a gesture of surrender.

Maybe Odin ought to crush his throat, here and now. If he let the man speak again, he risked another galdr ensnaring him. Still, Väinämöinen needed to sing to use his Art, so far as Odin could tell.

So Odin squeezed his grip until he felt Väinämöinen's neck begin to buckle. "Not good for your voice, I imagine. Consider that, before you utter one single note, song-crafter."

Eyes wide, Väinämöinen waved his hands in acknowledgment.

Odin released him, and the Kvenlander fell to his knees, gasping for air and seized by a fit of coughing. Odin's sympathies were limited.

Väinämöinen sucked in several breaths, coughing after each no doubt painful inhalation.

Odin knelt down beside him and put a hand on his shoulder. Then squeezed until the song-crafter yelped. "There is terrible beauty in your Art. Power, unlike aught that I have known before. But I find ... when face-to-face with a known enemy ... there is something to be said for having the strength of a snow bear. And the rage of one."

The song-crafter coughed, nodded, still raising a hand. "I am ..." He sucked in another breath. "Not your enemy."

"Surely you cannot claim to be my friend."

"Sometimes it is needful to take actions even friends mislike."

Odin shrugged. "Maybe that's why not all friendships last."

"Perhaps ... but an alliance ... of mutual benefit."

"Oh." Odin sniffed. "But you stole from me a rather precious commodity. You took ... *time*. Time neither I nor the world could afford for me to sit idle. In truth, I know not even how long you held me enthralled."

"But a few moons."

Odin groaned. As in more than one moon. And here he had dared hope it less than that. Maybe he ought to count himself lucky the song-crafter had not held him bound for several winters.

"You came to me seeking galdr," Väinämöinen said. "I can yet give you that which you seek. Songs to protect against arrows or swords or storms. Songs to ward you against fire or water. Against ice or cold ..."

Odin grimaced. Such secrets would be worth a great

deal. But then ... "I offered you riches for your knowledge and you attacked me."

"Yes, but I do not crave silver from your hoard, nor lands you would dole out. A price was offered, and a price was taken."

The price ... "My absence was your price. You wanted to do something you knew I would interfere with. What have you done, song-crafter? What have you wrought?"

Väinämöinen grinned now, so cocksure Odin considered cracking him across the jaw. A few lost teeth might serve as a reminder of who he was dealing with. "Naught which permanently impedes any of your machinations. You must decide ... whether your lost pride and your inconvenience are worth surrendering the chance at greater power. Faced with such a choice, where will you turn? How much is revenge worth?"

A question Odin had asked himself before now. No answer ever seemed sufficient. But Odin had already sacrificed far more than pride to secure his ultimate ends. No price truly seemed too high to pay when weighed against the very survival of mankind. Now, he leaned in close to Väinämöinen's face. "Teach me your songs. Show me the secrets, and I may yet count you among my allies. Believe me, song-crafter—you do not wish to be counted among my enemies."

Once again, the song-crafter smiled.

The Saga continues in *Days of Broken Oaths:*

https://books2read.com/daysbroken

SKALDS' TRIBE

Join the Skalds' Tribe and get access to exclusive reader rewards like *The Ragnarok Era Codex*, as well getting free books like *Darkness Forged* and notifications on release dates and sales.

https://www.mattlarkinbooks.com/go-runeblade/

Want maps, character bios, and background information on the Ragnarok Era? Look no further.

DAYS OF BROKEN OATHS EXCERPT

*S*tarkad's hand fell on her shoulder. "This place is little like aught you've known before."

Of that she had no doubt. Coming here might've been a mistake, but Starkad would not pass up this runeblade. Maybe even the last runeblade, he'd confided, though Hervor had no idea how he knew that. Either way, even if Rollaugr hadn't offered such a fortune to do this, Starkad would've come. And that meant Hervor would've come too.

In her absence, though, who knew what vileness Orvar-Oddr would wreak upon Sviarland? Upon those she cared for. The draug had tormented her without end. Coming here meant leaving him free to do so for any number of moons more. But she couldn't tell Starkad that. Couldn't tell anyone, save maybe Höfund, who stood gaping dumbly at the approaching port.

"It's magnificent," the half-jotunn mumbled. "Ain't never imagined so many people all clustered up tight like that. Gotta wonder how they keep from tripping over each other."

She frowned and cast a glance back at the rest of

Starkad's crew. Afrid Stonekicker stood a few feet from her, not even trying to hide her gaping at the approaching sight. Vebiorg was scowling like they sailed toward the gates of Hel itself. Who even knew what the others were thinking?

The ship itself was out of Kaunos, and her people were posing as merchants come to sell furs, with the captain and his sailors none the wiser as to their true purpose. Starkad and his men had loaded up crates of wolf pelts and snow bear skins all hunted from around Bjarmaland. A good enough plan to get in the city—assuming the port inspectors didn't take objection to the numerous weapons they bore.

Baruch assured them those inspectors would turn a blind eye to just about aught, provided Starkad handed over some silver coins.

Sure enough, as their ship docked at a pier, some official in black robes came bustling over, flanked by a pair of bodyguards. He strode on board the moment the crew had put down the gangplank. Immediately, he began spewing forth a stream of unintelligible foreign words. Was there a singular South Realmer tongue like Northern? Or did Miklagard and Valland have different languages?

She hadn't bothered to ask and it seemed pointless to pose the question now.

The official and the ship's captain exchanged words briefly, then the captain beckoned to Starkad. Hervor's lover tossed the official a jingling pouch. The official drew the strings to peer inside, nodded, and motioned for his guards to inspect the crates.

The two men popped one open, dug around in the wolf pelts. Muttered something to their employer. And just like that, they all turned and left. Didn't bother even checking the other crates, much less having a look at the passengers.

Starkad's crew had swords over their shoulders, axes hanging from their belts ... Afrid had a damn spear in her hand.

Nigh as Hervor could tell, all these Miklagardians cared about was their damn silver.

"It makes the city run," Baruch said, as if reading her mind.

"You mean the whole place runs on greed."

The Miklagardian shrugged. "Word is you used to be a pirate, Witchslayer."

She flashed him a half grin. "Point taken."

AUTHOR'S RAMBLINGS

The word "nightmare" comes from the old word "mare" (or "mara" in Norse and Old German). A mare was a night spirit or demon that visited frightening dreams on people. There are numerous other words for similar entities—alps or hags or kikimora. In fact, something along those lines exists in most folklores and mythologies for the simple reason that nightmares and sleep paralysis (also believed to be caused by maras) are found the world over.

Often, these creatures carry perverse sexual connotations and may be tied erotic dreams. That is, a mara is similar to or the same as a succubus or incubus. In modern fantasy, those sex demons have become erotic or comical in their renderings, but traditionally they were truly feared phenomenon believed to essentially rape their victims. A succubus would steal the seed of a man, pass it on to an incubus, who would then use it to impregnate a woman. The child of such a perverse union then became a cambion (a demon child in human form).

In *Days of Endless Night*, Starkad calls Ogn his mara, thinking she haunts him, but not realizing he had literally created a vengeful ghost waiting to get back at him. It seemed inevitable then, that he would eventually have to face the consequences of his mistakes. This led me to question what form, exactly, those nightmares would need to take and how they would be distinct.

Fairly early on, I settled on Ogn dragging Starkad along a nightmare tour of the Spirit Realm. By having him pass through different worlds, I hoped to make each dream sequence feel unique, while still retaining the essential horror and confusion of an endless nightmare.

I have always taken the tact that the supernatural here (in my Eschaton Cycle works like this one) is something to be dreaded. I think the danger of some fantasy is in making the supernatural fantastical in the truest sense of the word. I mean, that can be entertaining. It can be fun.

But you also risk losing the essence of how our ancestors actually felt about trolls or jotunnar or ghosts. Or mara. The thing is, these creatures were genuinely dreaded. People believed repeated visits from a succubus or mara would drain the victim's life away.

The world was a harsh place with large parts of it unknown and unknowable. And then you tack onto that the invisible realms of supernatural creatures. They weren't cuddly. They weren't things people went out and slayed. Or had tea with.

Actually that brings me to the hiidet (i.e. kobolds, i.e. goblins). Hopefully those came off in a light different than typical fantasy.

As always, when writing these things, to tell the truth about them, it becomes necessary for me to take it to places that make *me* uncomfortable. It made writing this volume a particular challenge, in much the same way *Days of Bloody Thrones* had been.

Days of Fading Dreams also features characters and settings from the Finnish epic *Kalevala*, such as Väinämöinen. I believe I mentioned in earlier works that the Ragnarok Era draws primary inspiration from Norse and Finnish sources. Most of the series thus far has focused on Norse sources, so it was exciting and refreshing for me to be able to finally give some hint of the things going on in Kvenland.

Väinämöinen himself is very similar to Odin, enough so that the two myths almost certainly influenced one another. Enough, even, that I had to give consideration to whether they would actually *be* the same person in my works. I do that, sometimes, merging characters or similar concepts to create a single, richer portrayal of the subject. In this case, though, I felt the interaction between the two would prove interesting enough to justify them being different people.

As always, I hope you liked the book.

Big thanks to Juhi and Regina for help and support, and to my cover designer.

Thank you for reading,
    Matt

P.S. Reviews are super important, especially to small presses like mine. Without reviews, small presses cannot get ads. It takes only a single line or two to make that difference. So if you liked this, please leave a review where you bought it!

Want to talk about the book? I'd love to hear from you. You can reach me at: matt@mattlarkinbooks.com

BOOKS BY MATT LARKIN

Gods of the Ragnarok Era

The Ragnarok Era is a dark fantasy retelling of Norse mythology, chronicling Odin's rise to godhood. If you love old legends, tragic mythology, and action-packed reads, check out The Ragnarok Era now!

https://www.mattlarkinbooks.com/series/ragnarok/

Legends of the Ragnarok Era

Legends of the Ragnarok Era expands on the world developed in The Ragnarok Era series by delivering dark tales outside the main series narrative. Fans of mythology should not miss this epic series.

https://www.mattlarkinbooks.com/series/ragnaroklegend/

Runeblade Saga

The Runeblade Saga is a series of dark fantasy sword and sorcery adventures set in the world of The Ragnarok Era. Filled with plenty of grim action, tragic heroes, and more than a bit of horror, these books are for fans of mythology and sword & sorcery alike.

https://www.mattlarkinbooks.com/series/runeblade/

For Juhi. You have no idea how much.

Made in the USA
Columbia, SC
21 April 2020

93252289R00159